HOWARD WALLACE, P.I.

HOWARD WALLACE, P.I.

by Casey Lyall

STERLING CHILDREN'S BOOKS

New York

STERLING CHILDREN'S BOOKS
New York

An Imprint of Sterling Publishing
1166 Avenue of the Americas
New York, NY 10036

ISBN 978-1-4549-1949-0

Distributed in Canada by Sterling Publishing
c/o Canadian Manda Group, 664 Annette Street
Toronto, Ontario, Canada M6S 2C8
Distributed in the United Kingdom by GMC Distribution Services
Castle Place, 166 High Street, Lewes, East Sussex, England BN7 1XU

For information about custom editions, special sales, and premium and
corporate purchases, please contact Sterling Special Sales at 800-805-5489 or
specialsales@sterlingpublishing.com.

Manufactured in the United States of America
Lot #:
2 4 6 8 10 9 7 5 3 1
06/16

www.sterlingpublishing.com

Wallace Investigations

Rules of Private Investigation

1. Work with what you've got.

2. Ask the right questions.

3. Know your surroundings.

4. Always have a cover story ready.

5. Blend in.

6. A bad plan is better than no plan.

7. Never underestimate your opponent.

8. Never tip your hand.

9. Don't get caught.

10. Pick your battles.

11. Don't leave a trail.

12. Everyone has a hook.

Chapter One

She didn't knock, just barged through the door like she owned the place. She did own it, but that was beside the point. I knew my rights, and privacy was at the top of the list. Planting herself in the middle of the room, she scowled as her eyes swept across the floor. Dirty cups and rogue pieces of laundry were noted and filed away on her mental list of grievances. With a hand clamped over her nose, she turned to me. "Howard, how many times do I have to ask you to clean your room?"

I told her to scram; a man's room is his castle.

Some mornings I should just keep my mouth shut.

"Howard Jamieson Wallace." The temperature in the room took a nosedive. "That's the first and last time you ever speak to me like that. I want this place spotless when you get home. Hurry up and get dressed—you're going to be late for school." With one last grimace at the offending mess, she turned on her heel and left. *Mothers.* She had a point, though. It was about time for me to check in at the office.

I pawed through the pile of clothes on the floor until I found a semi-presentable shirt. A half-eaten peanut butter sandwich from my sock drawer took care of breakfast. I pulled on my lucky coat, snagged my backpack, and headed out the front door.

Around the corner, in the garage, my ride waited patiently. A cobalt Cruiser passed down to me from the old man, he called her "Big Blue," and I saw no reason not to do the same. We'd patched her up more than a few times over the years, and she was now a two-wheeled Franken-bike held together by duct tape, twine, and baseball cards. Big Blue wouldn't win any pageants, but she was mine. The fact that she broke down like clockwork merely helped me keep track of time.

I strapped on my helmet, and we did a couple of turns in the driveway to warm up. Blue was never at her best first thing in the morning. I'd learned the hard way it didn't help to rush her. Lugging a forty-pound bike to school after she conked out with a cramp was a surefire way to end up late and stuck with detention. When her clanking settled down to a dull thump, we headed out. The direct route from my house to Grantleyville Middle School spanned eight blocks. It wasn't without complications, but the problem-free scenic tour added fifteen minutes to my commute. I could deal with a few bumps in the road if it meant logging extra Zs.

At the corner of Maple and Front, Big Blue took a breather while I creatively rearranged the contents of my backpack. After six long weeks of getting put through the ringer, I'd learned a few tricks.

Once my preparations were complete, we began the grueling trek up the giant hill also known as Maple Street. I knew what was waiting for me at the top. Blue shuddered as a tremor ran through my legs. Knowing was not the same as experiencing, and every time seemed to be a little bit worse. *Get it together, Howard.*

I braced for impact.

"Howie! Pull over."

Tim Grantley and Carl Dean leapt out of the bushes, blocking off the sidewalk. By far the largest, nastiest brutes in the eighth grade, both of them towered over me by at least a foot. Tim, the proud owner of more forehead than brains, had sprouted two individual facial hairs over the summer. He liked to stroke them while menacing his victims. I think he thought it was manly, but in reality, it was resulting in dry skin. Carl was the stoic flipside to Tim's posturing; a hulking behemoth carved out of granite. His face never gave any warning before he lashed out, making him a more dangerous foe than Tim. It was just my luck these two bruisers were my new morning welcoming committee.

Tim inherited this prime spot over the summer from his cousins, Greg and Jimmy Grantley. The town's founding family made it a point to look after their own—especially when it came to the low-hanging fruit of the family tree. Tim wasn't the brightest bulb, but in a sprawling clan like the Grantleys, they couldn't all be winners. Besides, smarts weren't exactly required in his line of work.

With the help of his henchman, Carl, Tim ran an extortion racket, plain and simple. In exchange for the choicest items from your lunch bag, they'd let you pass without injury. I'd tried declining once, but that'd resulted in me attempting to ride my bike with my underwear pulled up around my ears. It hadn't been much of a fight, as my only backup was a rusty pile of bolts on wheels. Now I was resigned to my daily shakedown.

Resting my feet on the sidewalk, I waited patiently as Tim swaggered up to me and Blue.

"Looked like you were planning to pass us by, Howie," he said, one finger stroking his lip.

I shook my head. "Wouldn't dream of it, Tim."

He grinned at me as he rested an elbow on Carl's plank-like shoulder. "That is good to hear, Howie, because I was concerned you were confused about your role in this little economic arrangement we have."

I sighed and dug a rumpled brown bag out of my backpack. "Nope, I am crystal clear."

Tim snatched it out of my hands and pulled out a chocolate chip cookie before tossing it back to Carl. "It's like Dolphinism," he said around a mouthful of delicious home-baked goods.

Carl looked up from nosing through the bag. "Darwinism," he said.

"Exactly." Tim nodded. "Survival of the fittest. We are of the fittest, ergo, we survive on your lunch."

Suffering through the indignity of their petty robbery was one thing. Having to listen to Tim's philosophizing kicked the experience up to a new level of torture. If he and Carl were the top of the food chain, the human race was doomed. I wondered briefly if the shaking under my feet was Blue's nerves or Charles Darwin rolling in his grave.

I reached down to wipe some stray cookie crumbs off Blue's fender. Life must be so simple for a goon. See cookies, steal cookies, eat cookies, repeat. If only I had the muscle mass to try it out.

"So, can I go?" I asked before looking up. Minimal eye contact was key in any Tim and Carl encounter.

Tim laughed out a loud, obnoxious honk. "He can't wait to get rid of us, eh, Carl?"

Carl didn't laugh. Carl never laughed.

"You're all fired up to leave us and hang out with your friends?" Tim feinted a punch, crowing with glee when I jerked back. "Two for flinching!" The shots to my shoulder nearly took me out of my seat. My sidekick didn't help matters by falling over in a dead faint. As I struggled to right Blue, Carl watched impassively and Tim shook his head.

"Howie, that is, unquestionably, the saddest bike I have ever seen." He jerked his head in dismissal. "Go on, get going."

Blue didn't need any more encouragement. I set my feet on the pedals, and, with a surprising burst of speed, we were on our way down the road. Tim and Carl tromped back into the bushes to enjoy the remainder of their morning of criminal pursuits.

With every inch of sidewalk added between me and the

dynamic duo, my pounding heart returned to its normal rhythm. Blue and I might know what to expect from those numbskulls, but that didn't make it any easier to choke down. We took a sharp turn onto Hillside Street and wobbled.

"Easy, Blue," I said, patting the handlebars of my skittish ride. She was getting too old for this kind of excitement. The stash of food weighing down my left pocket probably didn't help. My temporary solution to being accosted on a regular basis was to separate out the boring items from my lunch. As long as cookies and a sandwich were present, Tim and Carl never questioned if the bag was a little light. Today, I'd been left with an apple, carrots and two granola bars. I would survive, but a permanent solution had to be found—ideally something that gave them a taste of their own medicine. A person could only handle so much character building via public humiliation.

Big Blue and I trundled toward school, dignity trailing in our wake. Tim and Carl were relegated to the back burner for now. I had a full caseload to look after, and revenge was an expensive enterprise.

Chapter Two

After locking Blue up at the racks, I headed to the far corner of the schoolyard. I'd set up shop behind the outdoor equipment shed, under an ancient maple. It gave me plenty of privacy for nervous clients and plenty of shade for afternoon naps. My desk was an old wooden number the school had marked for the dump. A pickle bucket rescued from recycling filled in for the missing leg while a second bucket set against the trunk of the tree made for a nice chair. As far as offices went, it wasn't much, but real estate in my price range was hard to come by. I paid off Pete the custodian every Friday with a six-pack. (Five chocolate dipped and one jelly.) In return, he looked the other way when he mowed the yard and made sure no one ever cleared out my corner.

I swept the leaves off the top of the desk and set down my bag. No messages. That was hardly a surprise since I hadn't managed to find a secretary yet. Not that I had space for one anyway. Pulling the current case files from my bag, I took a seat. The early hour was taking its toll, and my eyes struggled to focus on the words in front of me. Tapping my feet on the ground, I fought against the inevitable. Resistance was futile. After rummaging around in my side drawer, I pulled out a pack of Juicy Smash gum and popped a piece in my mouth. I savored that first blast of flavor. I didn't know why I even tried to kick the habit. It had been twelve hours since my last piece—a personal record.

Refreshed, I read through the open files while I chewed. I had three active jobs on the books. The first one was a piece of cake. Our neighbor, Mrs. Peterson, had hired me to locate her missing cat, Gregory. A fat, mottled brown beast with a lazy eye, he wouldn't have wandered too far from his food source. I planned to walk around our street shaking his food bag while calling out to him about the dangers of outdoor living. Suburban raccoons could be ruthless.

A shadow fell across my desk, and I looked up to see a raven-haired dame staring down the sharp side of her nose at me.

"What can I do for you, doll face?" I asked and offered up my most charming grin.

Unmoved, she grimaced and pinched her lips, the words behind them too bitter to let loose. "I need your help," she spat out.

"Have a seat, toots," I gestured at the guest bucket, "and tell me all about it."

"Ugh," she groaned. "Cut it out, Howard, can you be serious for once?"

I straightened up in my chair, a flicker of irritation buzzing down my spine. I'm nothing if not a complete professional. "Now listen, lady, I don't know who you think you are but—"

"You've known me since kindergarten!" she yelled, her hands waving in the air. "This is ridiculous. I don't know what I was thinking." With a practiced flip of her hair, she turned to leave. I closed my eyes and counted to three. Funny how people were more willing to acknowledge your existence when they wanted something. I opened my eyes to catch a glimpse of Meredith's retreating form. You couldn't afford to be too choosy about prospective clients in my line of work, and Pete's donuts weren't going to pay for themselves. Even if this particular prospective client stuffed dirt down your pants throughout all of first grade.

"Meredith." I said, holding out a hand. "Come on. Don't be sore."

She looked back enough to pin me with some deadly side-eye. "Are you going to be serious?" she asked.

"Completely." At least until I could find something funny about working for one of Grantleyville Middle School's upper crust. "Please," I said, pointing to the guest bucket. "Have a seat."

She dismissed it with a sniff.

"I'll stand, thanks."

"Suit yourself." I got out a fresh notebook. "Now, tell me what's going on."

Glancing around nervously, Meredith stepped closer to the desk. "Someone's trying to blackmail me," she said.

I sat back in my seat and scratched my head. "With what?" I laughed. "You're a straight-A honors student with a record cleaner than a bar of soap." Meredith kept silent, and an idea began to squirm around in the back of my brain. I couldn't stop the smile that twitched across my lips.

"Unless there's more than meets the eye with Meredith Reddy," I said. "Did you cheat your way onto the Mathletes? Been skimming from the student council accounts?"

She cringed. I was on the right track with that last one. It always came down to money.

"What kind of mess have you gotten yourself into, Madame Treasurer?"

Meredith took a deep breath and squared her shoulders, locking me in a steely stare.

"Do you ever wonder why you're always by yourself in this disgusting hole you call your office?" she asked. "Because I'm starting to come up with a few good reasons."

That stung. My office area might be a little on the damp side, but it was nowhere close to disgusting. People paid good money for the kind of natural lighting I had. I guess it took a certain kind of person to appreciate its charms. I shrugged off Meredith's dig and got back to business.

"Start from the beginning."

"Yesterday afternoon, I went to get everything organized for the student council meeting this week, and I noticed the checkbook was missing. I thought I must have left it in the locker."

"Your locker?" I asked.

"The student council locker, but I checked mine as well. I found a note taped to it when I got there."

"On the student council locker?"

"*My* locker," she said, impatience underscoring every word. "Keep up."

"Do you have it on you?" I asked.

Meredith dug through the messenger bag resting on her

hip and pulled out a small white envelope. I snatched it from her outstretched hand and held it up for closer examination. Scrawled across the front in choppy, block letters was Meredith's name. A single sheet of paper lay folded up inside, covered in the same printing.

If you want the checks back, it read, *quit the student council by Friday's meeting. If you don't, have fun explaining to the student body where all their money went.*

I slid the note back in the envelope and looked up at Meredith. "Isn't that kind of an empty threat?" I asked. "I thought you needed the teacher advisor's signature on any check you wrote."

"You do," Meredith said, sinking down onto the guest bucket. "And lucky for this guy, Mr. Vannick signed the first three checks."

"Whose brilliant idea was that?"

"Mr. Vannick's." Meredith shrugged, and a small smile lifted the corner of her lips. "He thought it would make things easier," she said. "The Winter Dance is coming up, everything's agreed on, and this way I don't have to bug him when it's time to order stuff."

"How much money's in this account?" I asked. "Five hundred bucks?"

"Try five thousand," she said.

"*Five thou—*"

Meredith darted out of her seat and pressed a hand against my mouth to smother the rest of my outburst. "Perhaps now," she murmured, "would be a good time to talk about client confidentiality."

I pried her fingers off my lips. "I am a vault of juicy secrets," I said. "I can handle yours. How did the student council end up so flush?"

Meredith studied her hand for a moment before scrubbing it with the corner of her shirt. "The Parents' Association makes a generous donation every year. Half of the board members are Grantleys, and they like to make sure their kids have a healthy budget to play with."

"Even if it means sharing with the common folk?" The Grantleys weren't known for their altruism.

"Sacrifices must be made when one has a standard of living to maintain."

I straightened the papers Meredith had dislodged and tapped my pen against them. "I have to ask, why come to me?"

"I can't investigate it by myself. People would get suspicious." Meredith paced restlessly in front of the desk. "And I'm not going to give in."

"Why not go to Mr. Vannick?" I asked.

"And risk getting kicked out for losing the checks in the first place?" Meredith shook her head. "No way. I worked too hard for this. I'm the first seventh-grade officer on the student council in twenty years. Besides, everyone knows this is what you do. Can you help me or not?"

Sure I could. The question remained if I *would*. Solving a big bucks case like this was prime publicity, but swinging through the top branches of middle school society was not my favorite activity. I'd been there before and had the splinters to prove it.

Man up, Howard, I told myself. *A job's a job as long as it pays well.*

"It'll cost you," I said.

Meredith snorted. "I figured." She reached into her bag and pulled out another white envelope, slightly plumper than the last one. She tossed it onto the desk in front of me. "Will that do?"

I thumbed through the small wad of cash inside and nodded. Just enough to cover my pride. "It's a start," I said as I stuffed the money into the recesses of my coat. "Got your eye on any possible suspects?"

"Bradley Chen," she said immediately.

I paused in the middle of jotting down the name. "Why does that name sound familiar?"

"He ran against me for treasurer and lost. Since then he'll tell anyone who'll listen that I'm going to ruin the student council."

Sounded like Bradley was riding shotgun on the Bitter Bus. That was as good a motive as any. "Do you think he broke into your locker and stole them?"

"No," Meredith said, and a flush began to creep up her neck. "I think it might have been a bit easier for him than that."

"How so?"

"Bradley's always hanging around before our meetings," she said. "He's best friends with the president, Lisa Grantley— who also hates me, by the way." Meredith reached down to heft her bag onto the desk. "Bradley and I have almost identical bags and he 'accidentally' took mine when he left before the meeting started. I didn't notice until after we finished and he was in the hall with Delia."

"Delia?" The players in this game were multiplying.

"My best friend," Meredith said. "She always waits for me, and we walk home from school together."

"Meredith?" A small voice called from around the side of the equipment shed, followed by a petite blonde.

"That's her." She waved her friend over and then pointed back to me. "Howard's going to take my case, Delia."

"Oh," Delia said. "That's . . . nice." A ringing vote of confidence like that could go to my head.

The shrill sound of the bell rang out across the yard, signaling the start of the day.

"Could you meet me back here after school?" I asked. The sooner I solved this case, the better.

Meredith shook her head. "Can't. I have dance."

"Tomorrow morning, then," I said. "I'll want to ask both of you some more questions. In the meantime, write down your locker number and the student council one for me. I need to check for signs of tampering."

Meredith scribbled down the numbers and passed them over. A line of worry dug deep across her forehead. "Is that going to leave you enough time? Are you sure you'll be able to solve it by Friday?"

"Sure," I said. "I highly doubt there's some sort of criminal mastermind behind this."

"Let's hope not," Meredith said. "I can't afford for you to screw up."

With a case involving a Grantley, our student government, and five thousand big ones, neither could I.

Chapter Three

Wandering into my classroom, I ignored the chatter, my head still full of blackmail and intrigue.

"Howard Wallace!" The sharp voice cut through my musings like a whip. "I have called you three times." Ms. Kowalski, alleged seventh-grade teacher. I'd asked to see her credentials on the first day, and she'd refused to produce them. Our record of successful communication since then was low.

I approached the bench. "Yes, ma'am?"

She waved a familiar yellow folder at me. "What is this?"

I carefully considered the safest answer. "It would appear to be a yellow folder, ma'am." Ms. Kowalski sighed with gusto. It may not have been a sigh so much as deep breathing exercises to prepare her for the lecture to come.

"This, Howard, is your 'How I Spent My Summer Vacation' report. Please notice I said 'report' and not 'essay,' as the assignment dictated." She opened the file and began to read. "10 a.m. Subject entered break room and consumed one coffee and one strawberry jelly donut. 10:15 a.m. Subject returned to desk. 10:16 a.m. Subject began typing reports. 10:18 a.m. Subject attempted to distract investigator with trumped-up filing assignment." She flipped the folder closed and tapped the cover with one red-painted talon. "This is a surveillance report, Howard. Eight hours of minute-by-minute activity of a day at work with your father."

"I tried to be as thorough as I could, ma'am." It was probably the best report I'd done yet.

"You spent the *entire* summer at work with your father?"

"Not every day," I said, already annoyed by the judgment in her eyes. "Once I started my P.I. biz, I spent the rest of the summer on cases, but those files are classified."

"Classified," Ms. Kowalski muttered as she stared at the clock on the wall. I wasn't the only one counting down to the end of the day.

"Redo it as a proper essay, or you fail the assignment. I want you to give this note to your parents. They need to sign off on it." She held out the note and the file to me. As I took hold, she drew them closer and pulled me in until I could feel the heat of her dragon's breath on my face. Icy blue eyes lined by spiky black lashes drilled into mine. "A *proper* essay, Howard. I mean it." The woman had no appreciation of investigative excellence.

I strolled back to my seat and whipped out my notebook. The piercing voice of Lisa Grantley came over the speaker as she began reading the student news of the day. The fifteen minutes for attendance and morning announcements was prime time for reviewing case notes. I tuned Lisa out and turned my attention to more pressing matters.

Next on my list was Hillary Jenkins. She'd hired me on Friday to investigate the anonymous gifts someone kept leaving in her locker.

"Psst. Howard."

Flowers and candy, mostly. She said she hadn't minded at first, but the most recent one, a chocolate heart, melted all over her English paper. All of her suspects had alibis, so I was hoping a simple surveillance job would do the trick.

"Psssst. HOW-ard."

I shifted in my seat and turned my back to the whispers jabbing at me from across the aisle. Last on the roster was Scotty Harris; a sad-sack sixth grader who'd hired me to track down his lost (probably stolen) trumpet. If he didn't have it for band this week, he'd have to pay for the instrument . . . not to mention being bumped down to the recorder section, apparently a fate worse than trumpet player.

A pencil winged across my desk and landed on my notebook. I brushed it onto the floor and made a note to check out the local pawn shop on my way home.

"PSSSST! HOW—"

"What? What? WHAT?" I whirled around in my seat and came nose to nose with Ivy Mason: new girl, approximately fifty percent hair, fifty percent freckled nose (which she'd been poking into my business ever since she started classes last week). Leaning half out of her seat, almost across the aisle, she had a second pencil at the ready.

"What 'cha up to?"

"Nothing that concerns you," I said and turned back to my notes.

She leaned over even further, her chair now balancing precariously on one leg. "Is it detective stuff?" she asked. "Are you detecting right now? Can I see?"

"No," I said. "Beat it." There was precious little time to work in the morning and I wasn't going to waste it explaining the finer points of "detecting" to a newb with a passing fancy.

I heard the creak of her chair and looked in time to see Ivy pitch forward into the aisle. Shooting out a hand, I caught her and pushed her back toward her desk. For a second, I thought she was going to go too far and fall the other way, but after a couple of wobbles, her chair settled back into place.

"Eyes on your own paper," I said. My chair scraped across the floor as I faced the front, and Ms. Kowalski's laser-beam sight was on me in an instant.

"Howard Wallace," she said. "Kindly stop disrupting my class unless you wish to remain after school for detention."

Mumbling an apology, I cast a sideways glare at Ivy. She sat perfectly upright with an angelic expression plastered across her extremely nosy face. *Unbelievable.*

The rest of the morning passed without incident, and by lunch I was itching to get to work on Hillary's case. I had the perfect spot picked out for my surveillance—the girls' bathroom directly across the hall from Hillary's locker. It was always empty at lunchtime. The girls seemed to prefer to pile into the one beside the caf rather than trek all the way back here. After scouting the hallway to make sure the coast was clear, I pushed open the door and lurched to a halt. Ivy stood at the sink.

"What are you doing in here?" I asked.

"Using the GIRLS' bathroom," she said, making a show of washing her hands. "What are you doing here?"

"Working." I moved down the stalls, pushing in each door to check for other lurkers poised to ruin my stakeout.

Ivy turned off the tap and shook her hands in the air, sprinkling the counter with water. "Oh, good," she said. "I've been wanting to talk to you about that."

"Now's not a good time," I said and passed her a paper towel. "If you have a case, come see me during office hours."

"It's not about a case." She wadded up her paper towel and shot it at the garbage can. After hitting the rim, it bounced onto the floor. I kicked it out of my path and walked over to the exit.

"Then could you please leave?" I asked. "I need to use this door."

Ivy's eyes lit up. "What for?"

I did not have time for this. "None of your business, that's what for." I said. "If you're not gonna leave, stay out of my way." Squatting on the floor, I peered out the grate at the bottom of the door. Nope, not the right angle. I lay on my stomach and pressed my forehead against the metal. Perfect. A direct line of sight to Hillary's locker. All I had to do was wait for the mysterious gift-giver to show up.

A flutter of movement to the left caught my eye, and I turned to see Ivy depositing herself on to the floor beside me. "Scooch," she said. "I can't see."

"You don't need to," I said.

She wriggled over on her stomach and pressed her face against the grate next to mine. Piles of curly brown hair blocked my view and tickled my nose. "What are we looking for?" she asked.

Extracting myself from the mass of hair, I tugged on my coat until my pocket came into view. I pulled an apple out and shined it on my sleeve before taking a bite. "A lovesick locker bandit," I said.

"Awesome, I like that. It sounds like—ew, are you actually eating in here?"

"Yeah, it's lunchtime."

Ivy wrinkled her nose and looked around. "But, it's the bathroom." I followed her gaze, taking in the water-stained ceiling, faintly snot-colored walls, and cracked linoleum floor.

"Meh." I shrugged. "I've eaten in worse places."

Ivy's stomach rumbled as she gave my apple a considering look. I took a large bite out of it and raised an eyebrow at her. "Delicious," I said, managing to get the word out around a mouthful of fruit.

She scowled and looked back through the grate. "So this locker bandit, you got any suspects?"

"None that have panned out." I pushed Ivy's curls out of the way and craned my head, trying to see as far down the hall as I could. "I'm here to keep an eye out for any suspicious behavior." I turned to look at my intruder. "Which would be a lot easier if I didn't have an interfering lookie-loo horning in on the job."

Ivy laughed in my face. "Well, it's a good thing I'm here," she said.

"And why is that?"

"Because you're totally missing him. It's that guy right there." She pointed and I pressed back against the grate to see Alan Furst poking around in the locker above Hillary's. He pulled up the bottom panel and dropped a small parcel down into my client's locker. After carefully setting the panel back in place, he closed up his locker and walked away.

"Alan," I said. "He wasn't even on Hillary's list of possible suspects."

"Aw, poor Alan."

I scrambled up to my feet and pulled out my notebook to jot down this new development for Hillary's report.

Ivy stood up and stretched. "We make a pretty good team."

"Hm?" I put away my notebook and scrounged around in my pocket for a granola bar.

"Like partners, really," she said.

"Yeah." I was sure I'd stashed a bar somewhere. Oh, there. I peeled off the wrapper and took a big bite, then nearly choked when Ivy's words hit me. "Wait, what? What're you talking about?"

"I want to be your partner!" Ivy blurted out.

I shook my head. "Private investigation's not a team sport," I said. "I don't want a partner—I don't need one."

"Hey, I just solved a case for you, man," she said, her finger pointing in furious little jabs at the door.

"I would've solved it on my own if you hadn't distracted me."

"A partner would be a big help to someone who gets so easily distracted."

I snorted out a laugh. "A for effort, kid, but trust me, you don't want any part of this."

"I think I can make up my own mind, thanks," Ivy said. "C'mon, hear me out."

The bell rang, and I tossed my lunch garbage into the can. I'd already learned the hard way that partnerships were made to be broken. A wide-eyed tagalong wasn't going to change my mind about that.

"I know you're new, so you don't get it," I said. "I'm the last person you want to be friends with at this school. Now quit doggin' me."

Ivy stood rooted in place, blocking the only exit. Shouldering my way past, I heard her shout as I stalked out the door:

"Who said anything about friends?"

Chapter Four

I found Hillary at her locker after school and brought her up to speed on the case, handing over a healthy bill. She was surprised to hear Alan was the culprit but not overly upset. Maybe the guy had some hope yet. With that one off the books, it was time to move on to new business. I fished the paper from Meredith out of my pocket and double-checked the numbers. The student council locker was around the corner, and Meredith's was down the hall from it.

Locker number one was clean as a whistle, and I quickly moved on to number two. Meredith's locker looked exactly like all the others lining the hall: slightly bumpy door covered in industrial gray paint. No scrapes or bends indicating someone had tried to force it open. The lock itself looked intact. No visible signs of tampering. Maybe Meredith's bag swap theory was right. I was definitely scheduling a chat with Bradley for tomorrow.

I poked through my pockets until I located my pack of Juicy. Empty. That called for a pit stop at the office before making my way downtown. I headed out the door and across the yard. Next on my list was the case of Scotty and his missing trumpet. I had a feeling that one would be—

"What took you so long?"

I looked up to see Ivy sitting in my chair with her feet on my desk. She sported a wide smile, more proud of herself than any trespasser had the right to be. I stared her down until the grin faded, then shot a pointed look at the boots on my desk. She let out a low whistle and set her feet on the ground. "You're a touchy one, aren't you?" she murmured as she sidled past. The wad of gum in her mouth snapped noisily.

She'd been into my Juicy Smash stash.

I gestured to the guest bucket, and Ivy took a seat.

"This is quite the place you have here," she said. "Interesting style. What would you call it? Urban casual? Bucket chic?"

"What do you want, Ivy?" I asked as I settled myself behind the desk. "I've got work to do."

"I already told you. I want to be your partner."

"And I already told you, I'm not interested."

"I don't really think you've given the idea a fair chance." Ivy settled onto the guest bucket, getting cozy for the long haul. The girl was not giving up. Persistence in other people was always suspicious.

"Why?" I asked.

"Why what?"

"Why do you want to be my partner? We barely know each other." I dug through my desk drawer and pulled out a new pack. Three pieces missing. Apparently she was pushy *and* greedy.

"I know enough," she said. That's when I saw it. A little smirk, there and gone in a flash but around long enough to set my teeth on edge.

"Right." Arms crossed, I leaned back in my seat. "Who put you up to this?"

"What are you talking about?"

I'd seen far too many "innocent" faces in my lifetime to fall for Ivy's. "This is a poor excuse for a prank," I said. "Was it Tim? Miles?"

Ivy held up her hands. "Who? Howard, I—"

"What's the punch line? I take you on, we get a fake case, and you guys have a good laugh watching me run around trying to solve it?" I laughed once, short and bitter. "I don't think so."

"No. Jeez, Howard." She shook her head vehemently. "Paranoid much?"

"Then why?" My chair thudded back down on the ground as I jolted forward. "Why are you so hot to be a P.I.? Why do you want to work with me?"

Ivy stared at her feet, her eyebrows drawn together in a frown.

"C'mon, why?" She'd pushed it this far. I wasn't letting her go without an answer.

Something between a groan and a growl burst from Ivy, and the words came spilling out after it. "Because this town sucks!" she said. "There's nothing to do. I've lived here for two weeks, and I'm already bored out of my mind." Ivy slumped back in her seat, her temper fizzling out as quickly as it had sparked. "Do you know how hard it is to make friends in a town where everyone's known each other since birth? Pick a clique, any clique. I don't think so."

"Who said anything about friends?"

"Touché." She leaned forward on the bucket, intent on her pitch. "Okay, Howard. Real talk time. It's bad enough punishment that I've been exiled to no man's land—now I'm reduced to begging for entertainment. Bottom line is I'm stuck here, and you seem like the only kid who's found something cool to do."

I took a moment to digest her outburst. Grantleyville was definitely a few steps down from most places, excitement-wise. Me being in the same sentence as cool, however, gave me pause.

"It's not that cool," I said. "Most of the time it's boring. People get riled when you ask too many questions, so when it's not boring, it's usually messy."

"You're not gonna scare me off," Ivy said.

"Bravery is not valued over common sense here at Wallace Investigations," I said as something from Ivy's rant sent red flares through my brain. "What did you mean by 'punishment'?"

"It's a long story." She waved away the question. "Why are you the only kid in Grantleyville without a bestie?"

"That's a longer story." And not one I was inclined to share with an interloper. "What makes you think you'd be any good at investigation?"

Ivy held up four fingers and waggled them at me. "Hear me out, okay?" She lowered the first finger. "One, I'm smart. Two, I'm persistent. Three, I've got people skills. Something you're seriously in need of, by the way, so it'd be handy to have in a partner. Four, my dad's a cop, and I've picked up all kinds of investigative tips from him." Dropping her hand, she smiled.

"All I'm asking is for you to give me a chance."

She fell silent, waiting for me to respond.

I didn't need a partner. It wasn't like I was overrun with cases. It would only make things complicated—and aggravating . . .

. . . but interesting.

I'd had more fun arguing with Ivy in the last five minutes than I'd had in the last five months. Blue wasn't the best conversationalist. Having a partner would mean I could take on more cases. As *senior* partner, I could charge more.

I was delaying Ivy's departure by debating with myself. Telling her to buzz off was the most sensible thing to do, but I couldn't bring myself to say the words. A tiny knot travelled up from my stomach, unleashing whispers of doubt in my brain. My friendship-starved neurons were at war with my better business sense. *Get a grip, Howard.* I gave my head a shake.

Ivy sensed she was losing her audience and pulled a piece of paper from her pocket. "I brought my resume."

This should be good. I skimmed through the sheet she handed over. "Your hobbies are reading, spying, and skulking?"

"And baking."

"You've listed Sherlock Holmes as a reference." I didn't know whether to laugh or cry.

"Points for creativity! Come on, Howard," Ivy wheedled. "You know this is a great idea."

The kid was right about being persistent. She'd hound me until I said yes anyways. Not that I was saying yes.

"Maybe," I said, shaking my head even as I said the words. This was a terrible idea.

"Maybe, yes?"

"With conditions."

"Shocking."

"Temporary junior partner," I said. Ivy erupted in a fist-pumping chair dance. "Hey, hey, cool it. I said 'temporary.' We'll do a trial period for one week and see how it goes." I didn't see her sticking. She'd probably burn through her curiosity in a couple of days and wander off.

Ivy jumped up and grabbed my hand in an enthusiastic shake. "You won't regret this, partner!"

"Already do," I muttered.

She turned to leave and then stopped. "I have one question."

Of course she did. "Shoot."

"What's with the getup? Is that the company uniform or something?"

"What getup?"

She got a pained look and waved her fingers in the general direction of my lucky coat. I looked down and held out the sides.

"This? All P.I.s wear a trench coat."

"Dude, that's a brown bathrobe."

I shrugged and straightened out my sleeves. "First rule of private investigation, Ivy: work with what you've got."

"Noted!" She popped off a two-finger salute and began to walk away. "See you tomorrow, Howard Wallace."

I could hardly wait.

Chapter Five

I looked at my watch: enough time to squeeze in some work on Scotty's case before I was due home for dinner. Gathering up my files, I headed to the bike rack to retrieve Big Blue. She was leaning listlessly against the metal bars. A baleful air of loneliness and neglect unfurled from her in waves. The only bike left in an empty schoolyard. Cue the tumbleweeds.

I shook my head at her creaks of annoyance. "Chin up, Blue. Nobody likes a drama queen." I slapped on my helmet and we did a few warm-up laps of the parking lot before leaving. Frosty demeanor aside, Big Blue was never at her best late in the afternoon. Our destination sat only five minutes away: Marvin's on Main Street. Blue and I usually made it in ten minutes, but this time it took fifteen (punishment for the drama queen comment). I secured my pouty ride to the chain-link fence that lined the lot behind the store. Marvin's had the dubious honor of being the only pawnshop in Grantleyville. It was also one of the longest-running non-Grantley businesses, owned and operated by Mr. Marvin Parsons for the past fifty years.

I checked myself out in the window of the side door. It was always good practice to look professional for an interrogation. A scrawny kid trying to tame brown flyaway hair looked back at me. I was slightly taller than Ivy, but that wasn't saying much. Rumpled white shirt with a peanut butter stain on the hem, wrinkled jeans, scuffed blue sneakers, and a worn, brown terrycloth coat. At least my outfit screamed private eye if nothing else did. Squashing my hair down onto my forehead, I abandoned the attempt to spruce up my reflection. We were as good as we were gonna get.

I dug into my pocket for a piece of gum and headed around to the front entrance. A tinny bell jangled when I came through the door. Dust motes swam through the air with lazy abandon, and tiny shafts of light flickered as they fought through the years of grime on the front window. Decrepit merchandise lolled on the rickety metal shelves, any hope for another life given up long ago. Walking through Marvin's store was like walking through a graveyard of questionable life choices. A lacy, yellowed wedding dress with puffy sleeves hung in the corner. Mugs shaped in the heads of celebrities resided on a shelf on the back wall. Eight different Elvises took up the front row. There was a whole cabinet labeled "Junk Bought Off of the TV." It was one of my favorite places in all of Grantleyville.

Harsh, hacking coughs came from the small room behind the counter. I rang the ancient bell beside the cash register twice, loudly: once, to be heard before the wheezing could reach its crescendo, and the second time to show I meant business.

"Be right there," Marvin's voice rasped through the doorway. It had the gravelly tone of a larynx that had survived a lifetime of cheap cigarettes and poor ventilation.

Marvin wandered out and came shuffling up to the counter. I'd never learned his exact age but figured it could be anywhere from seventy to a hundred and five. His various vices over the years had preserved him to the point of human jerky. Coarse gray hair sprouted from his nose and ears, complementing the liver spots that dotted his bald head. In his prime, Marvin may have been a spiffy dresser. These days, a white tank top and black suspenders seemed to meet his requirements for business casual. He held up a pair of glasses, rearranged the dirt with a stained handkerchief, and peered through the thick lenses.

"Howard Wallace!" A dangerously phlegmy laugh erupted from his chest. "What brings you back to my fine establishment?"

I returned the grin and leaned an arm on the counter. "Working a case, Marvin."

"Ah, yes, the intrepid P.I." Marvin wiped his nose vigorously and stuffed the cloth back in his pocket. "Caught any more vandals lately?" He flashed a toothy, yellow smile at me when I shook my head and settled his bony elbows on the register.

"So, how can I help you?" he asked.

"I'm trying to chase down a valuable missing item for a client and I was hoping maybe it found its way here," I said.

"Well, anything I got in recently, I put over on the 'New and Hot' shelf." He chuckled as he waved a hand at the lone shelf beside the counter. A light sprinkling of dust covered most of the items, practically factory-new compared to the rest of the merchandise. Gleaming at me from its prime center spot was the jackpot.

"You got the 'Hot' part right, Marvin. You're harboring stolen merchandise here." I plucked the trumpet case from the shelf and strode back to the counter. Marvin's picture-perfect look of shock was the result of sixty-plus years of practice.

"Get outta town. Stolen merchandise? You kidding me?"

I turned the case around to face him. "See this little stamp here— G.M.S? That stands for Grantleyville Middle School."

"Howard," he groaned, "you expect me to be able to read teeny-tiny writing like that? An old man like me?"

I opened it up to show him the ID tag inside. "Property of Grantleyville Middle School. And see, under here, it says which student it belongs to for the year. Scotty Harris. Room 204."

Marvin shrugged. "Simple mistake. An oversight. Could have happened to anyone."

"I agree." I snapped the lid shut. "Scotty Harris made a mistake leaving his trumpet in the gym, and you made a mistake not vetting your merchandise." I began to lift the case off the counter when Marvin closed a hand over it.

"Mistake or not, I still paid good money for this thing."

"And I hope you learn from that. Now either I take the trumpet back to its rightful owner or you can explain to the police how it ended up here."

"Is that any way to talk to your first client?" Marvin scowled. "You know, I didn't have to hire you. Scrawny kid, coming in here, telling me you'll catch the bums painting up my windows. I could've kicked you to the curb."

"But you didn't," I said under my breath. Marvin was fond of this speech.

"But I didn't," he carried on. "I took a chance on you, and

now this is how you repay me? I'm just saying, I'm out of pocket for that piece. How am I gonna recoup the cost?" A mournful stare replaced the scowl. "I'm not as young as I used to be, you know. I gotta start thinking about retirement."

I fought back a smile. Never mind the fact that I had *solved* the vandal case for him. Marvin worked hard on his pathetic-old-man routine. A chuckle would only insult him. "Tell you what. How about I offer up a swap?"

Marvin crossed his arms and leaned against the doorframe. "I'm listening."

"You let me take the trumpet to Scotty, and in return I owe you a favor."

Shrewd eyes watched me as he chewed over that suggestion. "How do I know you'll keep your end of the bargain?"

I dug through my coat pockets with a wounded sigh. "Marvin, that hurts me." He shrugged his narrow shoulders and grinned as I pulled out one of my cards. "I'll write you an I.O.U., and you can give it back when you're ready to call it in."

He eyeballed the card and adjusted his speckled glasses for closer examination.

"Howard, that's a sticky note."

I scribbled down the debt and pressed it into his hand. "Times are tough all over, Marv. Take it or leave it."

He pocketed the card and spit into his other hand. "I'll take it." We shook on it, and Marvin squinted at me over the counter. "You know, a Grantley would never stoop to making deals with the likes of you," he said.

"I'd never stoop to making deals with a Grantley."

Marvin cackled long and loud before his laughter devolved into a wheezing cough. I slapped him on the back. Next to Blue and Pops, Marv was one of the few friends I had left in this town. I couldn't have him keeling over in front of me. He waved me off and straightened up, crowing at the ceiling. "Not today, you old coot." Marvin winked at me. "Not today." Satisfied he'd keep breathing a while longer, I headed to the door with my prize.

I didn't bother asking who'd brought him the trumpet. Even if he'd managed to get an accurate look at the culprit through his opaque lenses, Marvin would never rat on a future regular. Scotty would have to be happy with the return of his instrument minus the satisfaction of justice. Maybe this reprieve from the recorder section would teach him a valuable lesson about finders-keepers.

"You're good people, Howard," Marvin called after me as I blinked my way back into the sunlight.

Glad somebody thought so.

Chapter Six

Big Blue and I arrived home to find my old man parking his car in the garage. He eased his tall frame out of the seat and leaned an arm over the car door. "Howard, Blue." He gave a nod to each of us in turn. "How was your day?"

I pulled the note from Ms. Kowalski and the yellow folder from my bag and handed them over. After a brief perusal, he couldn't hold back a grin. "'Two p.m.,'" he read aloud, "'Subject exited back door and smoked one cigarette behind the dumpster.' You are good, Howard. I thought I got away with that." Pops closed the folder and considered the note again. "Tell you what," he said, handing them both back to me. "You write a *proper essay,* I'll check it over and your mother never has to hear about it . . . or the cigarette."

"Deal." We shook on it, and I shoved the incriminating evidence back in my bag.

"Besides getting busted for academic negligence, what else happened today?"

I popped Blue's kickstand and set her in her reserved parking spot, giving myself time to sort out which one of today's developments could be divulged. Once she was settled, I turned and hit Pops with the major headline. "The new girl asked to get in on the business. Wants to be my partner."

He paused, still reaching for his bag in the backseat, and shot a look at me over the top of the Volvo. "New girl?"

"Ivy Mason, four feet, ten inches, brown hair, brown eyes, no known aliases. Moved to Grantleyville a couple weeks ago. Keen to make her mark."

"Credentials?"

"None to speak of. Says her father's a cop and she picked up a thing or two along the way. I'm taking her on for a trial run, but I don't expect it'll work out."

He gave a low whistle and shut the car door. "Partner. That'll be a change—not to mention a blow to your gum supply."

"Junior partner," I pointed out. "If she even makes the cut. Plus, company rule: newbies bring their own gum."

"That's a solid rule." Pops nodded sagely as we exited the garage and headed toward the house. He paused on the driveway and stopped me with his briefcase. "Let's not count her out so quick. I think it'd be good for you to have someone to work with," he said with a suspiciously casual shrug. "And to have someone to hang out with again."

"What's that supposed to mean?" I shoved the case away from my chest. I'd had far too much Monday to deal with the direction this conversation was taking.

"Don't get all worked up, Howard," Pops sighed. "It's been months since Noah moved away and over a year since Miles—"

"He has nothing to do with this."

"All I'm saying is, gum concerns aside, it might be nice."

"I don't think anything to do with Ivy is ever *nice*," I said. "So far it's mostly frustrating and exhausting."

"I like her already," Pops said as he and I walked to the side door.

Inside, the usual pre-dinner chaos reigned. I'd no sooner set down my bag and hung up my coat than a hand snaked out and pulled me into the dining room. "Ho*weird*, you should have been home, like, thirty minutes ago. At least." Eileen Wallace: an unpredictable blond creature who was obnoxiously fourteen and irrationally annoyed at being related to me. She took after our mother in both looks and general aura of disapproval. A fistful of flatware was shoved into my hands. "It's your turn to set the table, freak. And Mom said no shop talk at dinner, so spend the next ten minutes coming up with something normal to talk about."

I wondered if Sam Spade got this much grief from his family. "I set the table yesterday," I called after Eileen as she stalked back to the kitchen. "It's your turn."

"Your own fault for being late," she said. "Next time, call."

Hard to do when your phone's been confiscated—indefinitely, according to my parents, or until I can learn appropriate usage. Why are there cameras in phones if not for taking surveillance photos?

After dinner, I sped through my homework (*proper* "How I Spent My Summer Vacation" *essay* included). I shoved my schoolbooks back in my bag and made sure Scotty's trumpet was in there for the next day. With that taken care of, I could finally get back to some real work. Grabbing the bag of cat food obtained from Mrs. Peterson, I hit the streets.

One hour and a pack of gum later, I'd walked the entire neighborhood. Shaking the kibble and calling "Here kitty, kitty!" had provided mixed results. Three cats followed me—none of them my target. I gave them each a handful of food to get 'em off my tail and on the slim chance the sight of other cats eating his fancy chow would bring Gregory out of hiding. A search of the surrounding porches, trees, and bushes proved equally useless.

The streetlights started to flicker on, and I headed back home. Maybe I could cram in some paperwork (and clean my room) before bed. My home office was in the backyard. It was a pretty sweet tree house that my old man and I'd built over the summer. More tree-adjacent, if you wanted to get specific. Neither of us was that stuck on heights. I stored all my files there and my main gum stash.

The inside was set up with Pops' old school desk, a rusty metal filing cabinet, and a camping lantern. In the corner sat a maroon easy chair rescued from the dump, surprisingly comfortable despite a few loose springs and suspicious dark stains. It was the place where I usually sat to work through a troubling case. Maps, notes, and surveillance photos covered every inch of wall space, making it a fire inspector's nightmare. Pops had also managed to land a couple photos of Humphrey Bogart as Sam Spade and Philip Marlowe to hang up. The detectives kept watch over the reference library: my two-shelf bookcase filled with secondhand detective novels. I waved at the guys on my way to the filing cabinet to retrieve the Harris file. After I finished an itemized bill for Scotty, I shut off the lamp and headed back in for the night.

Walking up to the house, I tossed the cat food bag absently from hand to hand. Shake. Thunk. Shake. Thunk. *Mewl.* I stopped in my tracks and tilted my head in the direction of the pitiful sound. "Gregory?"

Silence.

"You haven't thought this through, Gregory. There could be eagles out here." A soft meow came from behind a clump of peonies. "That's right. And probably wolves. Nobody's gonna think any less of you for coming in from the cold." I gave the food bag a little shake, and Gregory emerged, covered in dirt and leaves. He rubbed up against my calves, purring and meowing. "Life on the outside isn't for everyone, buddy." I bent down to give him some food and a scratch behind the ears. Hauling him up off the ground, I headed over to Mrs. Peterson's for delivery.

A shuffling noise caught my attention. I looked up to see a hand disappearing over the top of our gate. I ran over with all the speed I could muster while carrying a twenty-pound cat in my arms. Hitting the latch with one hand, I bumped the door open with my hip.

There was no one in sight.

I wandered down to the end of the driveway and scanned the sidewalks. The yellow glow of the streetlights illuminated an empty street. I listened for the sound of receding footsteps, but the quiet wisp of the wind through the trees told me what I already knew. Whoever had been there'd vanished. Gregory sank his claws into my arm and meowed pitifully. Our short jog had been the last straw of his big adventure. He was ready for a soft bed and a bowl full of food.

"Relax," I said. "I'm taking you home right now."

Slogging back up the driveway, I saw a glimmer of bright in the gathering dark. Taped onto the door of the gate, a little bit crooked and a lot crinkled, was a small white envelope. I pulled it down and held it out under the streetlight for closer examination. My name was scrawled across the front in very familiar block letters.

I removed the note from inside and read it out loud to Gregory.

"*Drop the Reddy case or else.*" I stuffed the letter into my pocket and looked around once more. "Or else what?" I called out. "Vagueness strikes fear in the heart of no one, you know." The mysterious note-leaver didn't jump out of the shadows with more specifics, so I continued across the lawn to Mrs. Peterson's.

"It's very interesting," I said to Gregory. "Not many people know that Meredith hired me. So how'd the blackmailer find out?" Gregory stared at me and began grooming his paw.

"I agree. We should definitely ask our client that tomorrow."

Chapter Seven

The next morning, I got up at the crack of 7 a.m. I planned to take the long way to school since I had people to see and no time for complications. Things went awry from the get-go when I couldn't find anything to wear. Then I remembered shoving all my clothes under the bed while cleaning up last night. That was the problem with cleaning: it was the best way to ruin a perfectly good system of pile organization. Luckily, I had two bananas browning on my bookshelf so I didn't have to waste any more time gathering breakfast.

Ten minutes later, I flew out the door and headed to the garage to retrieve Blue. My mother, with her bloodhound's nose for objectionable outerwear, appeared at the kitchen window. "You have a normal coat, Howard!" she yelled. I waved off her concerns as Blue and I completed our warm-up laps and lurched down the drive.

Once Blue realized we were taking the scenic route to school, she sailed down the sidewalk, clearly glad to have a Tim-and-Carl-free morning. We were making great time. It was a good thing too, because I had a packed schedule. First order of business was to find Scotty Harris and return his trumpet. I would accept his gratitude and praise and hand him my bill.

I didn't get much further in my plans because just then someone tried to kill me.

A kid on a scooter came out of nowhere, a blur of silver that cut across our path and nearly sent Blue and me into the street. I righted myself in the nick of time and hopped off the seat to check over my girl. Big Blue was as much in one piece as she ever was. "What's the big idea, kid?" I spun around to give him the full force of my glare. "You looking to be on the sidewalk or in it?"

He stood on a patch of lawn while his wheeled accomplice lay abandoned behind him. No more than eight years old, he had straw-colored hair mauled into an unfortunate bowl shape and a mile-wide stare. "Are you Howard Wallace?"

"Very nearly wasn't. What's it to you?"

"I heard from kids at school that you help people, when—

when they have a problem." A stammer and Bambi eyes. The kid was laying it on thick.

"What's your name?" I pulled out a pack of gum and shoved a piece in my mouth.

"Kevin."

"What school do you go to, Kevin?"

"Park Street Elementary. Sir." I couldn't help but be impressed that my reputation had progressed beyond the boundaries of Grantleyville Middle School.

"And what exactly is this problem you need my help with?"

The kid took a deep breath. "I need you to help me find my limited edition Spaceman Joe figurine with removable helmet and laser blaster. I haven't been able to find him since Sunday, and I'll never be able to replace him if I can't find him. I've written out a list of suspects and—"

"Kevin." I cut him off so we could get to the point. "Kevin. First things first. Do you have any money?" He looked confused, and I began to realize the downside of an elementary school following.

Bending down, I looked the little squirt in the eye. "Listen, I don't do pro bono. You hire my services, you pay my fees. My kid rate is five dollars a day plus expenses. Can you swing that?"

Kevin's face fell. "I spent all my money on Spaceman Joe,"

he said. Against my better judgment, I was starting to feel bad for the kid.

"Tell you what," I said. "You work on getting the dough together, then come find me. In the meantime, I'll keep my eyes peeled for the Spaceman."

"Thank you! I'll get you the money. I promise!" The kid was so grateful, you'd think I'd pulled the Spaceman out of thin air right then and there.

"I'm not making any guarantees," I said. "I'm saying if I see it lying on the ground, I'll try to remember to pick it up."

Kevin was already on his scooter, headed down the sidewalk. "I know you can find him! You're Howard Wallace!"

The soon-to-be broke Howard Wallace, if I kept being such a sucker.

I checked my watch and shook my head at Blue. Despite our plans to be early, we were skating toward on-time. Entirely too amused by the whole Kevin debacle, her handlebars tilted rakishly to one side. "Get your giggles out now, Blue." I hopped up and set my feet on the pedals. "Thanks to Spaceman Joe, we gotta hotfoot it the rest of the way."

Chapter Eight

I t wasn't pretty, but we made it. Grateful for a coat that was both lucky and absorbent, I mopped the sweat off my face with one sleeve as Blue and I coasted up the walk. I secured her to the shady end of the bike rack, hoping that by the end of the day she'd be recuperated enough to get us both home. Now to track down Scotty. As I scanned the schoolyard, looking for my client, the reedy, off-key notes of a recorder hit my ears. Jackpot.

Heading around to the back steps of the school, I snaked my way through the crowd of kids abandoning the area. The source of the musical blitz looked up morosely as I approached.

"'Hot Cross Buns.'" Scotty waved the tormented instrument at me. "I think I almost got it, don't you?" Telling Scotty his efforts sounded like a lovesick moose on helium struck me as someone else's job, so I settled for a noncommittal grunt.

He dumped the recorder back on the table and everyone in the schoolyard breathed a sigh of relief. "I realized I should probably start getting used to it," he said.

I grinned at Scotty and heaved my bag onto the bench beside him. "Your lack of confidence in my abilities both astounds and offends me." With a flourish, I pulled out the trumpet.

"You found it!" Scotty exclaimed, a wide smile stretching his cheeks. He leapt up and grabbed me in a bear hug. Scotty may have been a year younger than me, but he was a foot taller and twenty pounds of muscle heavier. It was not a comfortable hug.

"All right, all right." I pried myself loose and pulled an envelope out of my coat pocket. "Happy to be of assistance, kid. Here's my bill. Be sure to tell all your friends about Wallace Investigations." Scotty nodded absently, absorbed in his recovered treasure.

I strode back to my office, happy to be checking things off the to-do list at a brisk pace. The sound of angry voices reached me as I approached the equipment shed. Rounding the corner, I stopped short at the sight of Meredith and Ivy snarling at each other while Delia hung off to the side, as any sensible person would.

"I hired Howard Wallace. I only talk to *Howard Wallace.*" Meredith underscored each syllable with a forceful finger tap on my desk. I wasn't sure how long it would stand up to that abuse.

Charging into the fray, I held out my hands in peace. "Good morning, ladies. Glad to see you here so bright and early."

"It's about time." Meredith turned to me, the attack finger now pointed in my direction. "Can you make her leave? She's trying to feed us this crazy line that she's your partner now."

"Add a *temporary*, follow it with a *junior*, and that about sums it up," I said.

"Hah," Ivy said, triumph oozing out of every pore. "I told you so."

"Whatever, junior temp." Meredith sneered at Ivy, and I motioned for my associate to get out from behind my desk before she alienated our client any further.

Steering Meredith in the direction of the guest bucket, I set my bag down on the desk. "We need to talk," I said.

"I know, that's why I'm here." Meredith waved a hand behind her. "I brought Delia, as discussed."

"Great. First things first: who else knows you hired me?" I threw the question out there and scanned the girls' faces, looking for any kind of reaction. Delia hunched her shoulders and looked at the ground while Meredith froze in her seat.

"Why?" she asked.

"I got a visit from your blackmailer last night." I set the note on the desk and crossed my arms, leaning down to look Meredith in the eye.

"See, I was under the impression we were the only ones who knew about this case," I said. "I haven't told anyone, haven't even filled Ivy in yet, which leaves you two."

"It's Delia's fault," she snapped. Delia nodded, and Meredith's lip curled in disgust. "She wouldn't shut up about it in the cafeteria yesterday."

The harsh words cut deep. Delia shrank under Meredith's glare, looking more miserable by the second. "Funny," I said. "I wouldn't have pegged you for a loudmouth."

Delia frowned, and a mutinous look crept into her eyes. "I still think she's making a mistake. We should go to Mr. Vannick and explain the situation. He's a teacher. He'll help."

"Yes, I know that's what you think," Meredith said. "The whole cafeteria knows. And *you* know I'm not going to Mr. Vannick, because he couldn't care less about the student council. If it comes down to figuring out this problem or shutting us down, he'll choose door number two. Even worse, he might decide to kick me out."

She slowed down as her snit fit ran its course. "Delia only said I hired you, not what I hired you for, so at least there's that."

I settled into my chair and thought it over. "Okay, the blackmailer overhears your conversation, but unlike everyone else in the caf, actually knows what you guys are talking about. He or she decides to warn me off, and here we are. Not the end of the world, but let's be a little more careful from here on out, please."

Delia raised her hand.

"Uh, yes, Delia?"

"Isn't this bad though, the blackmailer knowing Meredith hired you? Should you keep investigating?"

Ivy came over to the desk and picked up the note to read. "I think it could be a good thing," she said. "If they know we're on the case, the pressure's on and they might start making mistakes." She tossed the letter back on the table. "That note is very unimaginative, by the way."

"Isn't it?" I turned to Ivy. "Here's your recap. Someone stole the student council checks from Meredith and is using them to make her quit. Our suspects are two eighth graders: Bradley Chen and Lisa Grantley."

"Madame President herself," Ivy said. "Scandal."

"How long did Bradley have your bag?" I asked.

"About twenty minutes," Delia said. "He came back before the meeting was over and demanded I get his bag for him." She tucked a lock of hair behind her ear and sniffed. "He was really rude about it too."

"Poor Delia was almost in tears by the time I came out." Meredith reached out to pat her friend's hand. "She hates it when people yell at her."

"And yet she's friends with you," Ivy muttered.

I cleared my throat and shot her a glare. She crossed her eyes and stuck out her tongue at me so quickly I thought I imagined it until I caught the bright smile that followed. This partnership thing was going swell.

I pointed my pen at Meredith. "When you came out of the meeting, what did Bradley say?"

"First he yelled at me about the stupid bag switch. He grabbed his bag out of my hands and tossed mine on the floor." Meredith sat up straight on the bucket, quivering with indignation. "Then, as if that wasn't bad enough, he said, loud enough for everyone to hear, 'If you're this careless with your own things, Meredith, I'd hate to see how you treat the school's money.'" She flung her hands out and scoffed. "And then he walked away. No, *strutted* is a better word. He was very pleased with himself."

Delia sidled up to my chair, leaning down toward me. "Everyone was talking about it afterward," she said, her voice at a low and confidential pitch. "It was awful."

People crowding my desk gave me hives, but I couldn't bring myself to snap at Meredith's beleaguered sidekick. Patting her on the arm, I steered her back to client territory, then flipped to my notes from yesterday. "We know Bradley's motives, but what do you think Lisa has against you?"

"Oh!" Delia's hand shot up.

"Yes, Delia."

"She and Bradley are best friends, so by principle—"

Meredith cut her off with an impatient huff. "I already told him that, Delia." She waved a hand at my notes. "The other reason is that I keep having to say no to her ideas for the Winter Dance. I mean, her plan for decorations alone would have blown our budget for the whole year." Meredith shrugged and shook her head. "But she's a Grantley, so the word no is like a foreign language to her."

I nodded sympathetically. I didn't envy Meredith, having to deal with a Grantley on a regular basis. Then again, I had Ivy now, so we all had our difficulties to bear. Meredith didn't strike me as the easiest person either, but Delia was still hanging in there. Which reminded me—

"Delia, where were you when Meredith found the note yesterday morning?"

"In the office."

My eyebrows shot up. "Really?"

"Oh, not like that." Delia blushed. "I volunteer there a few mornings a week helping Ms. Tomarelli with filing and stuff."

I made an extra note of that. You never knew when it would be handy to have someone on the inside. I closed my notebook with a snap and nodded at the girls.

"Thank you, ladies," I said. "You've been very helpful. We'll be in touch."

Meredith and Delia gathered up their bags and hurried out of the office. Another good reason not to upgrade the furniture; nobody lingered.

"That was good," I said, turning to Ivy, who hadn't moved from her spot leaning up against the shed. "We have some solid leads to chase down."

"Yeah, great," Ivy said. "Why didn't you tell me about this case yesterday? I felt like an idiot when they showed up this morning."

I opened my mouth and then closed it, unsure of what to say. Filling Ivy in hadn't been a priority until I found her and Meredith nearly coming to blows over my desk.

"It was need-to-know," I said. "Yesterday you didn't need know, but now you do."

"As your partner—" Ivy began.

"Junior partner," I interrupted. "Certain details are for senior partners only."

She grumbled, propelling herself off the wall in exasperation.

"Listen, kid, it's my agency, and I'll run it how I see fit." I bit back further arguments when I saw her ferocious expression. My old man's driveway pep talk nagged at me. This partnership business was murky territory, but I wasn't about to let it be said I didn't give it a fair shot. I had some fast talking to do if I was going to smooth things over.

"Tell you what," I said, grabbing at the first shiny idea that came to mind. "Come with me to interview Bradley, and I'll show you the interrogation ropes."

The bell rang, and kids started filing inside. I gathered up my stuff, ready to leave, but Ivy stayed planted in her spot. My idea wasn't shiny enough, apparently. "Oh, c'mon," I said. "Are you gonna be shirty or work this case with me?"

"Lucky for you," Ivy said as she sailed past me with her nose in the air, "I can multi-task."

Chapter Nine

I vy and I compared schedules at morning announcements and figured the best time to take a run at Bradley was over lunch. I did some fact-checking during English and confirmed he had the same break as us. Operation Interrogate Bradley was a go.

When the bell rang for lunch, people headed out to the caf, and I pulled Ivy aside to review our game plan. "It's a simple little chat. We want see how he reacts when we bring up Meredith," I said.

Ivy nodded. "I hear you." She edged in close. "So, who's good cop, and who's bad cop?"

My new partner had some highly unrealistic expectations for her new profession. "Ivy, we're not cops."

Her wide grin spread slowly from ear to ear. "Does that mean we both get to be bad cop?" She pulled a pack of gum from her pocket. "Relax," she said when she caught me squinting at the label. "This is from my own stash." She proceeded to unwrap a hunk of gum the size of a small apple and chomped it into submission. The scent of cotton candy wafted toward me.

"I think you'd have trouble being a convincing bad cop," I said. "Nobody'd be able to understand you over that wad." Ivy stuck her tongue out at me. The effect was a bit lopsided since the entire right side of her mouth was pulled tight by the gum tucked in her cheek. I tried to avoid staring at it. "Besides, like I said, we're not cops. It's merely a friendly chat with a possible criminal."

We wove our way through the throng of students. "I made some discreet inquiries during math class," I said. "Apparently, Bradley likes to spend his meal time in the east end."

"That's a prime spot. Big windows, extra chairs." Ivy punctuated her statement with a loud snap of her gum.

"It's also where the Drama Club hangs out," I said. "Bradley's their newest member."

"Student council to Drama Club. The guy likes a stage."

We neared the tables, and I decided it was best to lay down

some ground rules. Questioning suspects was tricky business, and you only had one shot to catch them off-guard. I put a hand on Ivy's arm to stop her from charging into the group.

"Time out, champ." I straightened her collar and smoothed out my own. "We're gonna run this smart, okay? Rule number four: always have a cover story ready. Follow my lead."

I spotted Bradley and his gang sprawled over the tables, limbs weighed down by the tedium of life offstage. I was unwillingly familiar with the world of theater, as my sister had always been heavily involved. It was a natural outlet for her dramatic tendencies. I had more mundane interests, like shaking down suspects.

Stepping up to the group, I zeroed in on our quarry. "Bradley Chen?"

Bradley flipped his hair out of his eyes. "Who wants to know?"

"I'm Howard, and this is Ivy. She's new. Her family moved here from the city."

Bradley leapt up from his seat and took Ivy's hand. "Oh, you poor, poor thing. Abandoned to the wilds of Grantleyville. How are you holding up?"

Ivy looked back at him solemnly. "It's been a struggle."

"I'm Ivy's student liaison, assigned to help her through the transition," I said. "We've been checking out different clubs this week, and Ivy said she was interested in acting. I heard you're the man to speak to."

"Excellent!" he said, perking up under the attention. "Do you have any experience?"

"I was in *The Music Man* and *Bye Bye Birdie* at my old school," Ivy said, smiling. "Recently I've been interested in more improv-based performances."

"Great." Bradley bobbed his head enthusiastically. "We do a lot of that in our group. The debate is still raging over what play to do this year, so auditions won't be until next month. You should come to a few of our meetings and see if you like it."

Ivy nodded, and I made my move. "Ivy's also interested in student government," I said. "You were involved with that last year, weren't you?"

He sniffed. "Hardly. Our student council is a joke. They let anyone in."

"Except for you, apparently."

Bradley crossed his arms and sucked in a breath. Ivy stomped on my foot on her way over to him. She laid a hand on his arm and gave it a gentle pat. "I know I'm new here," she said, "but I think I can say with confidence that it was their loss."

"Oh, believe me, it was. I had a million great ideas and a seventh grader got voted in over me." Bradley sagged down to take a seat on the bench. I leaned up against the side of the table.

"Isn't that how democracy works?" I asked. "The people vote in who they want?"

Rolling his eyes, Bradley directed his answer at Ivy. "The whole thing was rigged," he said, lowering his voice to a stage whisper. "Meredith Reddy, that girl who stole my spot, bought all her votes."

"Bought?" Ivy hadn't been kidding about her acting skills. Even I believed she was shocked.

"Cupcakes for everyone on the day of the election. Shameless." He shook his head. "I should've thought of it."

"So, really," I said, "you're mad that she out-underhanded you."

Bradley twisted around to face me. "I'm mad because she ruined my whole plan for eighth grade. My best friend, Lisa Grantley, *Student Council President?* We had it all worked out. We were going to rule the school and become legends."

"Sure," I said, sticking my hands in my pockets, finding it hard to pretend I wasn't enjoying myself. "Legends in bankruptcy court, maybe."

"Excuse me?" Bradley bristled. "What's that supposed to mean?"

"Word is, some of your plans were a bit pricey."

"More like amazing, and if Meredith's telling you any different—"

"I didn't say I'd heard that from Meredith," I said before Bradley could get himself worked up. His raised voice was starting to attract an audience, and he knew it.

"I wouldn't be surprised if you had," he said. "She's so threatened; she takes every opportunity to trash me."

"Slandering the competition," I whistled. "That is low."

"I can't imagine what you've been through," Ivy tutted.

"They shouldn't allow seventh-grade officers. They're too irresponsible for the position." Bradley turned to her. "No offense."

"None taken," Ivy replied with a little hand-pat of reassurance.

"Last week, she took my bag instead of hers. If she's not paying attention to her own possessions, how can we trust her with our money?"

"What happened after you mixed up bags?" I asked.

Bradley, caught up in his soapboxing, blinked. "Excuse me?"

"You walked off, realized you had someone else's bag, then what?" I jabbed a foot at the bag hanging off the back of his chair. "Did you poke through it and see if there was anything good?"

Bradley's face shuttered. "Of course not, I brought it back and had a chat with her and her little friend about carelessness." He looked over at Ivy and allowed a small smile to break through. "I have to get back to my friends, but I really hope you'll come by Drama Club. We're always happy to have new members."

"Super." Ivy said. "When do you meet?"

"Every Tuesday after school. You could start today."

"She'll see you then," I said, steering Ivy away from the group.

"I actually have to join?" she hissed at me.

"Shouldn't be a problem for the star of, what was it? *The Goodbye Bird*?"

"*Bye Bye Birdie*. And don't pretend you don't already have that info filed away," she said. "Besides, my stage days are in the past."

"Relax, it's temporary," I said. "We have to dig deeper on Bradley. Did you see his face when I asked him if he'd checked out Meredith's bag?"

Ivy nodded. "Sketchville. Population: Bradley."

"He's hiding something. You're going to find out what at the meeting."

"Okay." Shooting me a sideways glance, Ivy punched my arm.

"Ow! What was that for?"

"I can't believe you made me be good cop."

Chapter Ten

"Romeo, oh, Romeo. Something, something, Romeo." My junior partner was twirling around, holding what looked to be a scrap of paper towel in her hand.

"Ivy, cool it." We walked down the hall, surrounded by kids pushing past us, eager to be free for the day. I could think of a thousand ways to draw less attention to ourselves, none of which seemed to interest Ivy.

"What? I'm practicing." She flung her head back and fluttered the paper towel across her forehead. "Drama Club is literally around the corner, and I feel under-rehearsed."

I took out a piece of Juicy Smash and tossed it in my mouth before giving Ivy a once-over. "Play it the same way you did earlier. That was good."

Ivy cupped a hand to her ear. "Excuse me? What was that?"

"You heard me." I poked her in the shoulder. If I could get Ivy to concentrate, we had a chance of pulling this off. "For some reason, he likes you, so we have to use that to our advantage. Let's review the plan."

Ivy ticked off checkpoints in the air. "Get him comfortable. Get him talking."

"Preferably about Meredith and Lisa," I said.

"And if all else fails, get him mad and hope he trips up," Ivy said with a final twirl.

"No." I shook my head. "I'm serious, pay attention. We have an opportunity here to get the inside track with a suspect. Are you ready for that?"

"I'm so ready." Ivy straightened up, vibrating with excitement. "Lay the rest of the plan on me."

"You have to stay in his good books. Be his new best friend. Get him to confide."

"On it," Ivy said and then looked at me with growing suspicion. "What are you doing while I'm undercover?"

I smiled and snapped the gum in my mouth. "A little B&E on Bradley's locker. Maybe I'll get lucky and find the checks."

"Your assignment sounds like more fun," Ivy said, miffed. "How are you gonna break into his locker?"

We'd arrived at the classroom the Drama Club met in, and I steered Ivy toward the door.

"That knowledge is above your clearance level," I said.

"For now." Ivy shot off a small salute. "See you on the flipside, Howard Wallace."

"Remember: confidence, comfort, focus." I prayed this wouldn't end in disaster as she entered the classroom. Risking a peek inside, I spotted Bradley waving her over to the group of kids he was talking with. So far, so good. I hurried down the hallway to complete my own mission.

As I walked to my destination, I pulled a notebook out of my bag and flipped to the back. Earlier in the year, I'd made an important discovery in one of the janitor's closets Pete let me use from time to time (for an extra fee, of course). One of those times, I encountered a file he'd left out. It was a list of locker combinations for all the lockers at Grantleyville Middle School. Naturally, I borrowed it and made a copy. Or five. Valuable information like that couldn't go to waste.

"Sixty eight, sixty nine, seventy." I tapped a finger along the metal fronts while I tracked down Bradley's locker. After I found the combination on the list, it only took me two tries to get it open. Stepping back, I blew out a large bubble while I surveyed the contents of the locker.

Inside the door, an overflowing collage of pictures showcased the friendship of Bradley and Lisa. "Shrine" was probably a more accurate term. Bradley took his vow of best friendship very seriously. The contents of the locker were surprisingly jumbled. A pile of notebooks was rammed in haphazardly along with what looked like Drama Club notes. I was sifting through the papers when a flash of red caught my eye. Shoving all the books aside to get a clearer view, I nearly choked on my gum.

Taped to the back of the locker was a picture of Meredith. Bradley had drawn red horns on her head and given her a goatee. I carefully put everything back as I'd found it and closed the door.

I crowned myself the master of good timing when the instant I clicked the lock back into place, Mr. Vannick came around the corner and spotted me.

"What are you doing here?" He strode forward, and I tried to look as casual as possible.

"I'm waiting for a friend," I said.

Mr. Vannick slowed down as he got close enough for a better look. He studied me for a moment before recognition sparked in his eyes. "Wait a minute," he said. "You're Howard Wallace, right?"

That phrase always led to trouble when it came out of the mouths of adults.

"Yes," I said, slowly inching my way to the closest exit.

"I've heard about you." He stepped closer and glanced at Bradley's locker, its lock resting at a slightly crooked angle. "Is this your locker?"

"No, sir, I'm just—"

"Waiting for a friend," Mr. Vannick said. "Yes, you mentioned that."

Hunching my shoulders in my coat, I sidestepped away from Mr. Vannick and Bradley's locker. "She's probably done by now. I should get going."

He nodded and rocked back on his heels, hands clasped behind his back. "You do that, Howard." He leaned over me, the deep lines in his forehead each adding their own layer of disapproval. "Hanging around after school hours is ill-advised," he said. "For any student."

"Yes, sir," I said. "Understood, sir." I sped down the hall and relaxed my pace once I was out of sight. Time to meet up with Ivy and pursue some more ill-advised activities, all in the name of investigation.

Chapter Eleven

Thirty minutes later, I was cooling my heels on the back steps, still waiting for Ivy. Mr. Vannick never said anything about not hanging around *outside* the school. Good thing, too, since it looked like I wasn't going anywhere anytime soon.

The door slammed open, and Ivy staggered out, one hand plastered to her forehead and the other one grasping at the wall. "I survived," she gasped, sagging down to the ground. "Although I think I may have signed up to audition for the spring musical, and that's on you, pal."

"We'll deal with that later," I said. "What've you got for me?"

Ivy scooted forward to sit on my step. "Our friend Bradley can't say enough about the virtues of Lisa Grantley."

"That doesn't surprise me," I said. "He has a small shrine dedicated to her in his locker."

"Creeper."

"I think he prefers the term BFF." I leaned back against the concrete. "There was also a less-than-complimentary picture of our client on display."

Ivy nodded and stretched out her scrawny legs in front of her. "That's his other favorite topic of conversation. Meredith Reddy is 'the worst'!"

This was old news, staler by the minute. "Did you get anything useful out of him?"

"No, but . . ." Ivy trailed off and frowned.

"What?"

She picked idly at a loose thread at the bottom of her jeans before looking up again. "It was funny, watching him in Drama Club."

I nodded, waiting for her to continue.

"He hangs back and waits to see what everyone else is going to do," she said. "He never laughed at anything right away, just watched to see if anyone else was going to laugh first."

I got up from the steps and held out a hand to help Ivy up. "This is the kid who was going to 'rule the school'?"

"Exactly." She hopped up on her feet, and we headed for

the bike racks. "The more I hang out with him," Ivy said, "the less I think he could have planned this thing with Meredith on his own. Someone else planted the seed."

"Looks like tracking down Lisa has moved to the top of tomorrow's list," I said.

We came up to Big Blue, and Ivy hooted. "Nice ride," she said. "Did you make it yourself?"

"Ivy, meet Big Blue. Blue, meet my first major business regret." I unlocked Blue, and Ivy eyed her skeptically.

"Do you actually ride this thing or just push it around for show? Ow!" Blue had run over Ivy's foot as we started our warm-ups.

"Sorry, her eyesight's not what it used to be."

Ivy rubbed her foot and gave me the stink eye.

"Come on," I said. "It's time to get serious with your training."

Blue's cruising speed was the same as Ivy's walking speed, so we shared the sidewalk at an amiable pace. "We'll start downtown," I said, "to help you get the lay of the land."

"What, all five blocks of it?" Ivy snorted.

I shook my head. "If you want to be a P.I., you have to be familiar with where you work. Rule number three is 'know your surroundings.' You won't be able to track something down if you don't know where to start. And you definitely won't be able to get answers if you don't know the people."

Ivy gave an exaggerated bow with a sweep of her arm. "Then lead on, my friend. Show me the secrets of Snoresville."

I ignored that cheap shot and kept going. "Grantleyville was founded by the four Grantley siblings—Archibald, Henry, Marcus, and Rosalind—in 1869."

Staggering around the sidewalk, Ivy groaned. "Howard, what's with the history lesson? I heard all that junk from the Welcome Wagon lady." We turned onto Main Street.

"Fair enough," I said. "But did she tell you this town is still lousy with Grantleys? Look around, what do you see?"

Ivy scanned the main drag, taking in the tidy storefronts with their color-coordinated signs. "Grantley Hardware, Grantley Grocery, Grantley Menswear, Grantley Pharmacy . . . okay, yeah, that's a lot of Grantleys."

"Sure is," I said. "They still own half the town. There're a few independents like Marvin over there who thumb their nose at the establishment, but everyone else is in their pocket. Not much goes on here that the Grantleys don't know about."

Ivy looked delighted at this information. "Snoresville has a Mafia. I love it!"

"The point, Ivy," I said, hoping to redirect the lesson, "is that you have to know who will give you the goods and who'll turn you over to your folks. It's hard to work on an investigation when you're grounded."

"Speaking from experience?"

"You bet."

She began looking at the non-Grantley storefronts with greater interest. "So tell me who's willing to play ball."

I pointed out the pawnshop first—hard to miss, with its faded blue paneling and crooked front stoop. "There's Marvin. But watch out for him; he usually expects a favor in return. Don't promise anything you can't deliver." I motioned to Ivy's bag. "You should probably be writing this down." She rolled her eyes but went ahead and tugged out her notebook.

"Next is Mrs. Hernandez. She runs the bakery and the coffee shop." The tantalizing scent of fresh-baked Danishes drifted past my nose as we walked by. I resisted going in. My informants weren't prepared for the likes of Ivy on such short notice. "All the news makes its way through this door first," I said, shuffling her past the shop. "But if you go, give yourself lots of time. There's twenty minutes of gossip attached to every good piece of intel."

We neared the end of the road where the busy shops gave way to the peaceful, tree-lined streets of suburbia. The last stop on our tour was a squat building that'd laid its foundation before Grantleyville had a name. "Butcher shop," I said. "Ollie Benson, the assistant, runs a numbers game out the back. He's usually good for a tip or two if the boss is away. A pop and a chocolate bar."

Ivy paused and squinted at her notes. "And that is?"

"His usual fee."

She nodded and scribbled that information down. "Got it. Who else?"

Blue and I turned off Main Street and started coasting down Albert. "That's it. I'm not giving you all my sources on the first day. Now we go to the home office," I called out. "Keep up!"

Ivy chugged along behind me. "You know, I think I've figured out what bugs me about this town."

I looked back at her. "No movie theater?"

"Well, there's that. But no, it's the smell."

"What are you talking about?" I sniffed. "Grantleyville doesn't smell."

"Exactly! It always smelled in the city. I miss it. The street meat, the people, even the garbage! Chock-full of smells. And sounds! Here all you hear at night is the Snoresville Cricket Brigade."

"It's peaceful," I said, steering us toward my house.

"It's weird," she grumbled.

We trooped up the driveway, and I hustled Ivy into the garage. The last thing I needed was my mother or sister spotting her and making a big deal about me bringing a girl home. I didn't feel like explaining the finer points of our business relationship to them. I settled Blue in, and then Ivy and I headed to the home office.

She stopped in her tracks at the sight of it. I couldn't blame her. It was particularly striking in broad daylight. My old man and I were not what you would call master craftsmen. The building had a distinct lean we'd tried to cover up with a bright coat of paint. The gleam of fire engine red was broken up by the gaps between the boards. It creaked a little but was perfectly safe to be in if there were no high winds.

"I'm going to go out on a limb here and guess this is a Howard Wallace original."

I grinned and held the door open for her. "Frank Wallace and Son."

Once inside, Ivy started to nose around. She peered at my hand-drawn map of the town.

"You couldn't have bought one of these?"

"Not with customized shortcuts and escape routes. I'll help you make one for yourself."

"Oh, goody."

It was a small space to begin with, but having another person inside made it seem miniscule. The office had been designed for a party of one, and I doubted it could withstand a renovation. I hoped she wasn't expecting a desk.

"Hey, are these your old partners?" Ivy asked. "I thought you said you worked alone."

My gut twisted as I recognized the clump of photos she was pointing at. "No, and I do. That's Noah. He moved before the beginning of the summer."

She turned to face me, eyebrows raised in surprise. "Not a partner. Howard Wallace, was this individual actually your friend?"

"Can we move this along?" I asked, debating whether to take offense at the astonishment in her voice. Better to nip the conversation in the bud. We had way too much work to do to be wasting time with a trip down memory lane.

Ivy was back to examining the photos. "I didn't think you had any friends," she murmured.

"I don't," I said. "Remember that part where he moved?" Leaving me to deal with the perilous terrain of Grantleyville Middle School alone. Some things were unforgiveable. Ivy's sigh brought me out of my brooding.

"It sucks when people leave, doesn't it?" she mused.

Easy for her to say. "How would you know? You did the leaving."

"Not always."

That got my spidey-P.I. senses tingling. "What do you mean?" I asked, only to be met by a wall of deflection.

"Hey, who's this other guy?" Ivy was a fraction of an inch away from the photo. "He looks familiar."

"He's nobody. Come on. I'm not paying you to nose around."

"Actually, you are." Ivy blinked. "Is that Miles Fletcher? You know Miles Fletcher?"

"Used to know." I grabbed the photos off the wall, cursing myself for keeping the stupid things. They only reminded me of a couple of jerks who couldn't be bothered to stick around. Snaking the garbage can out from under the desk, I tossed them in.

"Past tense," I said. "Before he grew a foot and gained enough super jock powers to make everyone forget he used to be a nerd. Including him."

"*Hm.*" Ivy clucked her tongue, looking from me to the garbage can. "Anything you maybe wanna talk about, Howard?"

"You first."

She poked at the papers on the desk. "Isn't there more to this training thing?"

"That's what I thought. Sit here," I said, steering her closer to the ugly comfy chair. Maybe the smell would put a cap on the conversation.

Ivy plopped down on the seat, coughing when the cloud of stench rose up to envelop her.

"I want you to know that I'm here for you," she said, choking out the last words, "partner."

"Save it, sister, I know you're digging for dirt."

Ivy scrunched her nose at me, thwarted. "Miles is actually pretty cute," she mused. "Hey, do you think—"

"I will fire you if you finish that sentence," I said.

She opened her mouth to pepper me with more questions, but I cut her off before she could continue. "Listen, the training stuff is in my room. Sit tight, and keep your hands to yourself until I get back." Ivy slouched down in the chair and made a production of laying her hands carefully on her lap.

"This chair stinks, you know," she called out after me.

I made the trip into the house and back in less than three minutes. Ivy was already nose-deep in the filing cabinet. "Have you ever heard of alphabetization?" she asked. "Or a fancy new machine called a computer?" I walked over and gave the drawer a push. It shrieked and squealed, giving Ivy enough time to pull her hand out before it slammed shut with a crash.

"Hard to run a computer in here with no electricity," I said. "Besides, I like to keep all my files where I can see them." Not to mention my parents preferred to closely monitor my Internet usage. Apparently my search history had set off some alarm bells.

She leaned against the cabinet and tapped the top drawer. "What's the T and C surveillance file all about?"

"Something I'm working on my own. Keep out of it."

"You should get me my own filing cabinet then. And my own desk."

I bit back a sigh and handed her the training materials. "Junior partners get a notepad. End of story."

Ivy juggled the stack of movies I'd given her. "What's this?"

"The best way to teach yourself how to be a P.I. is to learn from the greats," I said. "Sam Spade in *The Maltese Falcon*, Philip Marlowe in *The Big Sleep*, and Nick and Nora Charles in *The Thin Man*."

"You're not serious." Ivy's grin faded. "Howard Wallace. There are over fifteen movies here."

"Roughly thirty hours of intense theory and methodology," I said. "These guys will teach you how to talk, how to tail a suspect, the top interrogation techniques. You name it, they'll show you the best way to do it."

Ivy looked dubiously at the pile. "I have a feeling the only thing these are going to help explain is you."

"I used them to come up with the Rules," I said as I plopped a sheet of paper on top of the stack. "Memorize them. All members of Wallace Investigations must follow these rules to achieve investigative success."

Ivy scanned the list with a critical eye. "Did these movies also help you come up with the dress code?"

"Out," I said. "Be at the school office early so we can get cracking on Lisa."

"Yes, sir." She clicked her heels together and nodded off a salute while balancing the load in her arms. I followed her out the door and was watching her leave when a flurry of activity in the kitchen window caught my eye. Groaning, I shook my head as I marched to the back door. Better to catch my mother before she caught Ivy.

The door opened the instant I reached for the handle. My mother appeared in the doorway, craning her head around me in an attempt to see the sidewalk. "Howard, does your friend want to stay for supper?"

"If you feed her, she'll keep coming back."

"Howard Wallace, don't be rude. It would be nice for us to get to know your new friend."

"Quit calling her that. She's not my friend. She's my partner."

Her encouraging smile faded at that bit of news. "Partner. Joined your 'detective agency' type partner?" I pushed past her into the kitchen and took off my coat.

"Yeah, Ivy Mason. She got it in her head she wants to be a P.I., so I cut her a break."

"Ivy was here?" My old man had wandered into the kitchen and was sniffing at the various pots on the stove. "Why didn't you invite her for dinner?"

My mother turned to him in disbelief. "You know about Ivy? How do you know about her and I don't?"

"Howard's second rule of private investigation, dear," Pops smiled. "Ask the right questions."

Chapter Twelve

The next morning got off to a bumpy start. Two days of hard labor, trekking back and forth to school, put Blue in a foul mood. She got that way every Wednesday. I managed to coax her down the driveway only to have her drop her chain once we hit the sidewalk. "Blue!" I said. "Pull yourself together." It took me a few minutes to set everything back to rights, and then I gave her a dollop of hard truth.

"Here's the thing, Big Blue. You're a bike. You're built to carry people around. That's never going to change, so you're gonna have to get it square in that rusty noggin of yours." I patted her headlamp affectionately. "We're only halfway through the week, and I still have business to conduct. It'd be nice if you could try to maintain at least a small level of professionalism.

Do that for me and you can have the weekend off. Deal?"

She didn't fall over or bust a tire, so I figured it was safe to assume we had an understanding. The rest of the ride was smooth until we hit Maple Street. Blue and I slowed down so I could adjust my lunch. We were nearly at the corner when I heard a familiar voice calling my name.

"Howard Wallace! Wait!"

Blue rattled to a stop, and I turned to see Ivy huffing down the sidewalk after me. This was the last thing I needed: a partner who didn't stick to a plan. "Weren't we supposed to meet at school?" I asked, frowning. It was one thing for me to deal with Tim and Carl every morning. I had no intention of dropping off innocent bystanders at their feet.

"Good morning to you too, Howard."

"How did you even find me?" I hadn't been training her that well.

Ivy leaned against the stop sign, fanning herself with the edges of her coat. "I'm a crazy good detective," she said. "Plus I stopped by your house first, and your mom told me you'd be going this way."

"Ratted out by my own mother. The shame." The woman had no idea what she'd done.

"I'm going to pretend you said, 'Hey, Ivy! Nice to have

some company on the walk to school.'" Ivy hopped away from her post and twirled on the sidewalk. "So," she asked. "What do you think?" It was a bright, balmy October day and Ivy had on a neon green raincoat with yellow daisies on it.

The misfortune of having an older sister had taught me a number of hard and fast life lessons. Never to comment on fashion choices was in the top five. Besides, appropriate outerwear was the least of my concerns at this point. I grabbed a piece of gum from my pocket and chewed it as I decided the best avenue of avoidance. On all fronts.

She nudged me with her elbow. "Every P.I. wears a trench coat, right?"

"Is that what that is?" Good thing I'd never answered the question.

Ivy sulked and yanked on my sleeve. "First of all, look who's talking, bathrobe boy. And what was that you told me? 'Work with what you've got'?"

At least she'd been listening.

"Don't expect to be doing any surveillance in that getup."

"Right, because the girl in the raincoat would look so out of place next to the boy in the loungewear."

"Brown loungewear, Ivy," I said. "Earth tones blend."

Ivy started up the hill, flapping the sides of her coat as she went. "I'll tell you one thing," she said. "Plastic doesn't breathe. It is Sweat City under here."

Her wardrobe complaints turned to white noise as my brain whipped through different scenarios, trying to figure out how to redirect Ivy and get her out of the line of fire. We might have been spotted by now. If I stuck around as a distraction, Ivy had a chance at getting to school uninterrupted. I slid off Blue and wheeled her alongside my clueless partner. "You should cut over to Hickory Street." I said, grasping at straws. "More trees, lots of shade."

"Trying to get rid of me?" Ivy asked.

We were getting close to the danger zone, but Ivy still had time to turn back. "Only looking out for my partner," I said.

"Aw, how sweet," she said. "But why would I take a detour when we're almost there?"

"This route has its drawbacks," I said.

Right on cue, Tim and Carl surged out of the bushes, and Ivy yelped in alarm.

"Morning, Howie, you know the drill—" Tim cut off abruptly when he noticed Ivy standing beside me. "What a surprise," he said in a long drawl. "Howie's got a friend."

With a miniscule shake of my head, I shot Ivy a hard look that I hoped said, *Keep quiet and follow my lead.*

"Did you get a lady friend to go with your lady cycle?" Tim asked.

"Excuse me?" Ivy snapped. Cringing inwardly, I made a note to work on more effective silent eye communication.

"No offense to you, Freckles," he said, "but it's most unusual to see our pal Howard in the company of other humans."

I rummaged through my bag for my lunch. "I've got what you want, Tim. Leave her alone, okay?"

Tim sucked in a breath and hocked a wad of spit at my feet. "No can do, Howie," he said. "She wants to pass, she's gotta pay the toll."

Ivy put her hand up. "Toll?"

"Your lunch." Tim pointed at her bag and grinned.

"For real?" she asked. "This is your thing? Ambushing kids and stealing their lunches? Way to aim low in life, guys."

"Ivy," I hissed at her as quietly as possible, but it didn't matter. She was on a roll.

"Who actually puts up with this ridiculousness?"

Tim pointed at me, and Carl coughed. Ivy's mouth fell open when she caught sight of the lunch bag in my grasp. She put a hand on her backpack and shook her head. "No, no way."

I passed my lunch over to Tim. "How about we call it even with that, eh, guys? Give her a pass."

Tim gestured for Ivy's bag. "We do not disseminate."

"Discriminate," Carl said.

"Or that." Tim took a step toward Ivy. "Equal stealing from all."

A stubborn look clouded Ivy's face, and she held her ground.

"Ivy, just do it," I pleaded. "We'll get you something else to eat."

"That's not the point," she said, holding her bag tight to her chest. "I refuse to hand over my lunch simply because these idiots said so."

I closed my eyes briefly. "Ivy, I'm begging you."

She swung her gaze back and forth between me and the moron patrol. Her chin lifted a fraction of an inch. "No."

Tim smiled. He never encountered much opposition and was enjoying the change of pace. "If you don't pay the lunch toll," he said. "You have to pay the W toll."

Ivy stared at Tim, bewilderment crowding out her anger. "What's the W toll?"

Tim cracked his knuckles, and he and Carl stepped forward as one. I groaned, and Ivy turned to me.

"Seriously, what's the W toll?"

... .⁻ ⁻⁻ ⁻..⁻. ... .⁻⁻. .⁻ ⁻.. .

Five minutes later, we were back on our route, picking our underwear out of our teeth.

"If you'd listened to me even a little bit, this could have been avoided." I shook my head as I kept a shaken-up Blue on a steady course. "Junior partner," I said. "You're supposed to follow my lead."

Plucking at her pants, Ivy did a high-stepping dance down the sidewalk. "In all my life," she said, "I've never been given a wedgie. I thought that only happened in movies. Thanks, Howard, for helping me reach that horrible milestone."

I snorted out a laugh and carried on coaxing Blue along to school. Ivy had gotten off easy. I turned to tell her so, only to see she wasn't there. Looking back, I saw her parked a few feet behind, glaring at me.

"It's not funny," she said. "Why didn't you do anything to stop those guys?"

She didn't get it at all. "There's no stopping Tim and Carl," I said. "There's just surviving them."

Ivy shook her head. "How is giving in the only option? There were two of us and two of them."

"Ivy, c'mon," I said, throwing my hands out to highlight my less-than-impressive frame. "Two of us barely equals one of them."

"My dad says a bully can only push you around for as long as you let them."

Parents give the worst advice. "No offense, Ivy, but your dad is full of it."

Her head snapped up, indignant anger boiling out of her. I held up a hand before she could defend her father's shortsighted words of wisdom.

"Listen," I said. "There are two kinds of bullies in this world: those who are trying it on for size and those who mean business."

Disbelief ran rampant over Ivy's face. "Oh, and Tim and Carl mean business?"

"They own a franchise."

Ivy started walking again, kicking along a small pebble as she went. "I'm trying to get this straight. You let them take your lunch? Like, every day?"

"Not every day," I said. "Sometimes I take the long way to school. Or I get a ride." But detours and rides weren't always possible, and the truth of it was—there would always be a Tim and Carl. Guys like that can pop up anywhere. Every encounter with them I made it through was another check in the endurance column.

Ivy sniffed and made a little *hmm* noise before going back to kicking her rock.

"What?" I asked.

"Nothing."

"Spit it out."

"It's disappointing, that's all," Ivy shrugged. "I never figured you for a pushover."

I slammed on the brakes, and Blue's gears screeched in protest. It was bad enough Ivy had witnessed my daily ordeal. I didn't need her judging me for it. "I am *not* a pushover," I said. "I'm smart." When did being sensible suddenly become being a pushover? "Who asked you to come along, anyway?" I demanded. "If you'd listened to me and stuck to the plan, you'd be at school and we'd both be able to walk properly."

"So now it's my fault?"

"I'm not saying it's not."

"Howard!"

Blue creaked and shuddered while Ivy glared at me. Now I was getting it from both sides. Guilt squirmed in my stomach. "I'm sorry, okay? I should have at least warned you what you were walking into."

"That would've been nice," Ivy said. "Why didn't you?"

"And have you go charging in there to give them a piece of your mind? You think that would have gone better than this did?"

"We'll never know, will we?" she sniffed.

"You gotta understand that I'll deal with Tim and Carl in my own way, in my own time," I said. "In a way that is not saying no to their faces when they're in possession of giant fists." I held up my own considerably smaller fists for emphasis.

Ivy looked unconvinced, but the dynamic of the delicate balance between thugs and their targets wasn't easily explained to those on the outside. I set my feet back on Blue's pedals and started forward again. Maybe something good could come of this, what Ms. Kowalski would call a "teaching moment." If Ivy was determined to join the P.I. game, she'd have to get used to all the dirty tricks that came with it.

"This was an important lesson for you this morning," I said.

"Explain that one to me."

"Rule number ten," I said. "Pick your battles. You've got to be in control of a situation and only fight when you know you can win."

"And you think Tim and Carl—" Ivy trailed off.

"Are not a battle worth fighting right now," I said. "We have more important things on our plate. Like Meredith's case." We arrived at the bike racks, and I locked Blue up tight. "You want in on this gig, you have to learn how to compartmentalize."

"I get what you're saying," Ivy said. "Right now, I'm really annoyed at you and kind of want to punch you, but you're saying we have to work on the case, so I should save it for later."

Hmm.

"I think I should explain it again," I said.

"You could try."

As we rounded the corner to the office, Ivy froze. "Howard," she said. "Your desk!" The whole place was in shambles. All the buckets were toppled over, and the desk was lying butter side down in the dirt. I sighed. You came to expect this sort of thing when you didn't have a lock. Or a door. Or walls, for that matter.

"Grab the guest chair, would you?" I got busy turning the desk back over and resettling my own bucket to its optimal lean against the tree.

Ivy brushed dirt off of the desktop. "Who would've done this? There's not an evil rival agency around, is there?"

"This isn't an unusual scene to walk into," I said. "Could've been squirrels. Or delinquents. Or—delinquent squirrels."

Ivy shook her head and wiped off her hands on her jeans. "And you're okay with your stuff being trashed on a regular basis?"

I pulled open a desk drawer. Juicy Smash stash unharmed. At least I could chalk up one win to the morning's numerous losses. "It is what it is," I said. "People are going to mess with me no matter what. Having an outdoor office kind of invites this sort of thing."

She flopped down onto the guest bucket. "Sadly enough, that's only the second weirdest thing I've learned about you this morning."

I reached into the drawer and reorganized the packs back into neat, orderly rows.

"Listen," I said. "It's not like I keep important files here. It's a pretty small price to pay for, you know, not having to pay for anything."

"Haven't you ever thought about setting up some sort of security system?" Ivy asked.

"I did," I said, "but then I took on a partner. I could probably swing it if I fired her."

"A private eye and a comedian." She tapped a finger on the desk. "You'll need new business cards. Sorry, business sticky notes."

People always had to take a jab at the sticky notes. "Enough with the gags," I said. "We've got a case to solve and not a lot of time to do it."

"What's the plan?" Ivy asked.

"It's time to meet the president."

Chapter Thirteen

Getting close enough to talk to Lisa proved to be an impossible task. Every time we approached, one of her entourage blocked us off.

When lunch finally shuffled around, we were tired, frustrated, and no closer to our goal. Ivy and I were working on our game plan when Meredith appeared. Seething, she threw down a white envelope on my lunch tray.

"What exactly am I paying you for?"

Ivy snatched up the envelope, and I plucked it out of her fingers. After reading the contents, I scoffed. "This is nothing," I said to Meredith. "They're trying to scare you off."

Meredith grabbed the note back and scrunched it up into a ball. "It doesn't sound like 'nothing,' Howard. *I have more than one way to get what I want.'* It sounds like they're getting serious."

"There are rumors," Delia said, popping out from behind Meredith. "People are saying Meredith hired you to find dirt on Lisa because she wants to be president."

Three pairs of eyes turned to stare at Meredith.

"Well, obviously, yes, I do," she said. "But not until next year. It's all part of my twenty-year plan. First, I win—"

"We had an interesting chat with Bradley yesterday," I interjected, wary of how long a description of a twenty-year plan would last. "He mentioned something about you buying your votes with baked goods."

"Oh, please, he wishes he thought of that." Meredith rolled her eyes and flicked her hair back. "The cupcakes were just a bonus. I came up with a good strategy, and I earned my place fair and square."

"Keep reminding yourself about that. Whoever's behind this," I said, pointing at the scrunched-up envelope in her hands, "they're all about cheats and shortcuts, and that's what's gonna get them caught."

Meredith's shoulders slumped. "I hope so. Have you had a chance to talk to Lisa yet?"

Ivy and I shook our heads.

"It's been a little difficult tracking her down."

"She has volleyball practice after school," Meredith said. "Try catching her then." She jerked her head at Delia, and they headed toward the student council table. Ivy and I watched as Meredith pushed her way through Lisa's crowd of admirers to take up residence on one of the chairs.

"Do you have a twenty-year plan?" Ivy asked around a mouthful of granola bar.

"Kid, we're lucky when I have a twenty-minute plan."

... .‾ ‾‾ ‾..‾. ... .‾‾. .‾ ‾.. .

Due to circumstances beyond my control, Ivy and I were late getting to the gymnasium.

"I still don't understand why you couldn't say 'Thank you, Ms. Kowalski' when she handed back your essay," Ivy said.

"Because," I said, "she smiled at me."

Ivy stopped in mid-rush down the hallway. "What?"

"Smiled like she'd won. I didn't like it." It was only October, and I wasn't keen on the idea that Ms. Kowalski believed she was the early victor in our war, especially not if I had to deal with her in homeroom *and* English. I'd flipped through the essay and pointed out all the spots where my surveillance report provided superior information. She downgraded me from a B- to a C, but at least we were back on even ground.

Ivy snorted and shook her head. "You're ridiculous."

I straightened my sleeve cuff and considered that. "Maybe," I said. "But I also think I'm winning."

We snuck through the gym door and stood in the shadow of the bleachers. Practice was well underway, and not much could be heard over the squeak of shoes, the thumping of the ball, and the girls on the sidelines shouting encouragement at the players. The coach was pacing the edge of the court, yelling out instructions. When he turned, I caught a glimpse of his face. Mr. Vannick. The man was everywhere lately.

Ivy poked me in the side. "There's Lisa." She pointed out a tall blonde, laughing and high-fiving another player.

One of the greatest investigative advantages is the opportunity to observe your subjects when they're unaware of being watched. People behave more like themselves when immersed in their natural environment. Lisa reigned supreme over her home court. She smiled and bounced around. She soaked up the attention. The girl was all sunshine—until you looked into her eyes.

Lisa Grantley had a predator's eyes. They were razor-sharp, constantly tracking those around her. Her head whipped to the right as one of her teammates tripped, missing the ball and allowing a point. The other team cheered. Lisa's eyes narrowed.

Her mouth tightened before she called out a rallying cry to her team. The ball came back into play.

I saw the moment she went for blood. The girl who'd scored stumbled on the other side of the net and the ball came Lisa's way. She leapt up and spiked it down, hard, into the other player's back. Lisa smiled as the girl face-planted and then quickly rearranged her features into a look of shock and dismay.

"Lisa," Mr. Vannick shouted. "That's not how we play here. What were you thinking?"

Lisa trotted over to the sidelines, her head bowed. "I'm sorry, Mr. V, it was an accident. I didn't think she'd be so slow." She snuck a look at her victim, and triumph glinted in her eyes.

"It's okay, Mr. V, I'm fine." The fallen player staggered to her feet and waved a hand at Mr. Vannick. I recognized her look of resignation well. Better to take a blow from Lisa as public punishment than rat on her and face worse away from prying eyes.

Mr. Vannick wasn't convinced. "I don't ever want to see behavior like that again or you're suspended from the team," he said to Lisa. "Do you understand?" Lisa nodded meekly, and Mr. Vannick blew his whistle. "That's it for today."

The team scuttled off in a huddle while Lisa prowled

after them. It wasn't merely one player; she had the whole team under her thumb. I grabbed Ivy, and we snuck off to wait outside the girls' locker room.

Despite the power play we'd just witnessed, Ivy was all excitement.

"I'm meeting Grantley royalty," she said, pacing around the hallway, patting her cheeks and forehead with every turn. "I've got so many emotions running through me right now. Wonder. Excitement. Anxiety."

I had always found sarcasm to be much less amusing when you were on the receiving end. "Are you done?" I asked from my post, leaning against the wall.

"Almost," Ivy tilted her head to the side. "How's my hair?"

"Brown."

"Right on."

"Remember, you're taking the lead on this," I said. "There's no way Lisa's talking to me when she thinks I'm Team Meredith. We've only got one shot at her. Make it count."

"I'm not going to screw this up, Howard," Ivy said, all of her teasing light fading away. "I won't let you down."

Lisa Grantley came barreling out into the hall and stopped short when she spotted me.

"You."

I grinned. "Me."

Her lip curled and she straightened every blue-blooded inch in her body. "I have nothing to say to you."

Snaking a pack of Juicy from my pocket, I cocked my head toward Ivy. "You might change your mind when you find out who my friend here is."

That put a hitch in her stride. It's a rare person who can resist a hint of mystery. She glanced at Ivy.

"Ivy Mason," I said as I wrangled a piece of gum from the battered pack, "meet Lisa Grantley. Lisa, meet the newest reporter for the Grantleyville Middle School Blog."

Lisa plastered on the winning smile every Grantley was taught at birth. She gave Ivy a slow once-over and tapped her fingers on her hip. "Mason," she said. "You moved here with your dad, right? You're staying with your grandmother on Greenfield Road."

"Yes," Ivy said slowly. "How did you know that?"

"I'm a Grantley," she said. "It's my job to know what goes on in our town." Lisa brushed at her bangs and smirked. "You should know that."

I pushed myself away from the wall and strolled over to stand beside my partner. "Ivy's doing a feature piece on all the student council members."

"I thought I'd start with you," Ivy jumped in. "You *are* the president, after all."

"Okay, but only for a few minutes," Lisa said and smoothed out her shirt. "I'm meeting someone soon."

Ivy dug her notebook out of her bag and flipped through, pretending to consult her notes.

"You come from a long line of Grantleys who held student government positions," she said. "What's it like being part of such an impressive legacy?"

Lisa posed prettily, regardless of the fact neither of us had a camera. She spoke as though reading from the Grantley Book of Public Relations. "It's an honor, not only to have been chosen by my fellow classmates but also to be keeping the tradition of Grantley leadership alive."

Ivy stared at Lisa, processing the weirdness spewing out of her mouth. Lisa dropped her pose, and irritation flickered across her face. "Aren't you going to write that down?"

"Oh, right." Ivy made a few scribbles on her paper. "Next question: How do you view the council's role in our school?"

"The council is vitally important to our school," Lisa said, her eyes growing brighter as she warmed to the topic. "We are the face, heart, and mind of the student body. We are the agents of change and the custodians of student welfare—seriously, you're not writing any of this down? This is good stuff."

Ivy passed her notebook over to Lisa. "Maybe you should do it. I'd hate to miss anything."

Lisa snatched the pen from Ivy and began scrawling across the page, muttering to herself. I tamped down the impulse to jump in. Ivy may have different methods than me, but she was still getting results. After underlining her last few sentences, Lisa tossed the notebook back to Ivy and gave the pen an appreciative glance before pocketing it. "That should cover everything," she said. "I'd work on my interview skills if I were you. Not everyone's as approachable as I am."

Ivy cleared her throat and peeked over at me. I nodded. Time to take things up a notch.

"One more question, if you don't mind," Ivy began. "You made quite a few promises in your campaign speech." Lisa stiffened as Ivy flicked through her pages again. "A coffee bar in the cafeteria and a dance every month. Neither of these has happened so far. Can you tell me when you'll actually follow through?"

Advancing on Ivy, Lisa towered over her target. I tensed, ready to intercept if necessary.

"I believe I said I would *lobby* for a coffee bar. I'm currently in talks with the vice principal about it. As for the dances," she said, smacking the corner of Ivy's notebook. "There's been *resistance* with regard to spending our money on what the students want. Some members are excessively concerned with the 'budget.'" She did air quotes around the word "budget" like it was a made-up issue.

"Do you have any comments on the rumors about friction between you and Meredith Reddy?" Ivy asked.

"What is this?" Lisa charged toward me. "What's Meredith up to? I know she hired you."

I held up my hands to ward her off. "I don't know what you're talking about."

Lisa and I stood nose to nose as she backed me into the wall. "I am not someone you want to mess with. Make me ask again and I won't do it nicely. Why are you really here, Howard Wallace?"

Ivy stepped in between Lisa and me, clutching her notebook as a shield. "He helped track you down for the interview. That's all. Why don't you look at this as an opportunity to set the record straight? Since everyone's talking about you guys anyway."

Lisa laughed bitterly. "You want me to confirm to everyone that we're fighting? To say that Meredith is the worst mistake this school ever made and that she's ruining everything? Not a chance." A small smile crept out, the same one she wore after beaning that girl with a volleyball. "Off the record?"

Ivy nodded enthusiastically.

"I don't think that she'll be with us much longer," Lisa said.

"I really hope you mean not with you on the student council as opposed to with us in this world," I said, only halfway joking. Grantleys were bred for ruthlessness.

"Very funny, Howard," Lisa said.

"Who'd replace her?" I asked. "Bradley Chen?"

Lisa smiled broadly and looked at her bare wrist. "Why, look at the time," she said. "I'm late for my meeting." She flounced off down the hall.

I looked over at Ivy, who had pulled out a new pen to finish up the last of her notes. "What do you think?"

"Honestly?" She tapped her notebook against her leg. "I think it doesn't add up."

"Explain, young apprentice."

"First of all, check out this handwriting." Ivy flipped to the page Lisa has left her answers on. "Way too messy to be the same person behind those tidy little blackmail notes."

I hated to admit it, but I was impressed. "Nice bit of business," I said. "Getting a sample of her writing like that."

"Told you I'd picked up some tricks," Ivy crowed. "Super pro detective, right here."

"Calm down, super pro," I said, ducking her high fives. "What else isn't working for you?"

"Telling us she thinks Meredith's going to get the boot?" Ivy snorted. "If she was really behind it, don't you think she'd have played it closer to the vest?" She gulped down the rest of her laughter. "Unless she is, and she's actually that dense."

"Or that confident we can't tie her to it," I said. "But I agree, there's more going on here." We started walking down the hall, and I thought about our interviews over the last couple days.

"Bradley's not strong enough to have done this on his own, but Lisa's too reckless. She was ready to take my head off back there," I said. "This plan's been acted out carefully and methodically. Whoever our blackmailer is must have some serious restraint."

"You think there's someone else involved?"

"It's entirely possible." I nodded. "There must be another angle we haven't considered yet. We need to start looking in other directions."

Turning the corner, I ran smack into the iron bulk of Mr. Vannick. He pinned me with a face-melting glare. "Howard Wallace. What do you think you're doing?"

Chapter Fourteen

I vy and I tried to look innocent as Mr. Vannick repeated the question.

"School is done," he said. "What are you doing here?"

"Interviewing Lisa Grantley for the GMS blog," Ivy said. Mr. Vannick looked around, and we all noted the distinct lack of Lisa in the area. "We just finished," she amended.

Mr. Vannick pointed at the exit. "Well, get going," he said. "Seriously, kids are supposed to *want* to leave when the bell rings."

We made it halfway down the hall when Mr. Vannick called out.

"Oh, and Howard? Is that your blue bike at the racks?"

I nodded slowly. "Yes, sir."

"You should be careful about leaving it out there for so

long after hours." He walked toward me, measuring out his words with each step. "It would be unfortunate if something were to happen to it."

"Yes, sir." I bit off the last syllable and held my ground. I didn't like his tone.

"Okay, then. On your way." Pivoting on his heel, he walked back to his classroom. A buzz sounded from his pocket, and he pulled out his phone. "Hello."

Ivy grabbed my sleeve and pulled me closer to the side door.

"Hold on a sec," I said, leaning forward, trying to catch a snippet of Mr. Vannick's conversation.

"Howard, what are you doing?" she whispered.

"You were listening to that, right?" I crept down the hall, closer to Mr. Vannick's classroom. "Am I the only one who thought it was weird?"

"He's a teacher," Ivy said, tightening her grip on my arm. "It's kind of their job to make sure we're not doing things we're not supposed to do." She shot a look at the open door of the classroom. "Like eavesdropping."

"First of all," I said, keeping my voice low. "Eavesdropping is a top-tier detective skill, so get used to that. Second, tell me how that crack about Blue adds up."

"Yeah, that was strange," she said. "I don't know how he'd think anyone would steal your disaster of a bike."

"Hey. Nobody insults Blue but me."

"My apologies to Blue," Ivy said. "On both fronts."

We were close enough to the room that we could hear Mr. Vannick's voice as it drifted out into the hallway.

"I'm leaving right now."

I risked a quick peek around the doorframe. Leaning against his desk, Mr. Vannick had one hand on his phone, the other on a frayed, red lunch bag. His battered briefcase sat lopsided on top of a squat garbage can. Ivy poked me in the side, and I motioned for her to stay back.

"I know it's late, but you know it's Wednesday. Volleyball practice." Sighing, Mr. Vannick reached down to grab his case. "No, Friday is the student council meeting." Another sigh. "There's nothing I can do about it. I drew the short straw this year."

I felt something nudging at my feet. Looking down, I saw Ivy crouched on the floor, straining to get a glimpse inside the classroom.

"Ivy," I hissed. She had the nerve to look up and shush me.

"It's a complete waste of time," Mr. Vannick said. "If I could get out of it, I would." He turned to grab his coat off his chair, knocking the briefcase against the desk as he leaned. The locks on the case split open, allowing papers to tumble out. A loud groan travelled across the room. "Honey, I have to go. I'll see you soon." Mr. Vannick shoved his phone back in his pocket and scrubbed a hand through his hair. When he bent to gather up the papers and bags, I took that as our cue to leave. Pulling Ivy up to her feet, I hustled her back down the hall and out the side door.

"The weirdness keeps piling up around Mr. Vannick," I said to Ivy. "We need to ask him some questions tomorrow."

"I can see that going super well," she said as we walked along the side of the school to the back lot. "Hey, isn't that Lisa and Bradley?" Ivy pointed.

Our suspects were locked in what looked like a heated argument. Both of them were yelling, and Lisa was flailing her arms.

She caught sight of us peering at them over the recycling bins and said something to Bradley. His head whipped around to look over, and she grabbed his arm, propelling him down the sidewalk, away from the school.

"Come on," I said. "Show's over, and I want to stop off at the office for some more gum before we go home."

Mr. Vannick's phone call needled at my brain. "Do you

think all the teachers feel that way about the student council, or just Mr. Vannick?"

"Don't know," Ivy shrugged, "but if he's this aggravated six weeks into it, imagine what a beast he's gonna be by June." She stopped in her tracks and gasped. "Howard, look!"

I looked around. "What? It's not a spaceman, is it?"

"What?" Ivy poked at me. "No, the squirrels have gotten into the office again." She walked through the debris. "Honestly, this is ridiculous."

I looked around at the carnage. The buckets and the desk were in a tumbled heap. The desk drawers had been pulled out and scattered over the ground. I lifted a couple to look underneath them. No Juicy. There was, however, a piece of paper with familiar block writing on it.

"Not squirrels," I said, "unless they've learned to write." I passed the note to Ivy.

"*I warned you once. I don't like repeating myself. Quit the Reddy case,*" she read. "*Or else.*" She handed it back to me. "Again, very vague."

"Yes," I agreed. "But it means we're doing something right."

"Oh, really?"

"Yup," I said. "I've never been threatened *and* vandalized before." I grinned at Ivy. "I must be getting good."

Chapter Fifteen

I bounced around the next morning brimming with confidence. My investigative skills had pushed someone to the point of destruction and extortion. *Someone* knew I was on their trail. The fact that they found me disconcerting enough to take such measures warmed my heart.

I whistled on my way into the kitchen. Eileen sat at the table, wolfing down her breakfast in deference to the fact that she was already late for school. She looked up when I entered the room, and a muscle in her right cheek began to twitch.

"What's got you in such a good mood?" she demanded.

"Coercion," I said.

She stared at me for a few seconds and then got up to toss

her dishes in the sink, shaking her head. "You are a freak and a half."

"A freak who gets results," I said, pouring a wave of cereal into my bowl. "That extra half is spare awesome."

"I'm leaving now," Eileen said. "Keep talking to the people who care."

I looked around the empty kitchen. "I'm going to solve a case today," I said to my cereal.

After making short work of my breakfast, I headed out to the garage to snag Big Blue. Invigorated by my enthusiasm, Blue zipped up the street with the speed of a bike half her age. Even Tim and Carl had a hard time putting a dent in my mood. They made a solid effort, relieving me not only of my lunch but my gum funds as well. I was undaunted. There'd be more where that came from once Ivy and I solved this case and started raking in the clients.

Ivy was idling on the bike rack when we arrived, bright green raincoat on full display. I had a sinking feeling this behavior marked the beginnings of a habit.

"Rule number five: blend," I said.

"I'm sorry; I don't understand cryptic muttering this early in the morning. What are you talking about?"

"If you're going to lurk around the bike racks, you should

probably get a bike." I secured Blue and looked up at Ivy. "Did we have a meeting?"

"No, we have a problem," she said.

"Good. I hate meetings."

"You're hilarious." Ivy vaulted off the rack and fell into step beside me. "You know what else is hilarious? The new rumor someone started about Meredith. It's a doozy."

I took a moment to digest that piece of information. "Have you seen her yet today?"

"She's waiting in the office—"

A ripe curse interrupted Ivy, and we turned to see Mr. Vannick struggling up the sidewalk, trying to keep a hold on his various possessions. The travel mug in his left hand tipped precariously as he kept one finger looped through his old lunch bag. His right hand gripped the handle of his worn briefcase. The coat he had flung over his arm was sliding to the ground despite his best efforts to pin it to his side. The case banged against his leg, and both locks broke open. Papers streamed out on to the pavement. Mr. Vannick's curses began to increase in volume and creativity. Ivy and I jogged over.

"Need some help, Mr. Vannick?" I asked.

He looked up with a jerk and fumbled his mug in the

process. Black coffee poured out in a wave over his shoes and the papers strewn across the sidewalk. "No, no, no!" he cried.

We crouched down to rescue what we could out of the path of the creeping coffee puddle. Mr. Vannick grimaced at the mess, then threw his coat on top of it and started to mop it up.

"I'm glad we ran into you, sir," I said. He grunted and wrung his coat out over the grass. "My friend Ivy is new here, and she has some questions about our student council."

She nodded and gave him a big smile. "My old school didn't have one, and I love that the students here are so actively involved. It's not often we get to be part of the decision-making process."

Mr. Vannick snorted. "All they're deciding on is whether or not to have balloons at whatever silly dance is happening. It's an hour every Friday that's a waste of everyone's time."

"Oh," Ivy said. "I'd heard it described a little differently."

He looked at her and gave his head a shake. "No, yeah, you're right. It's a great program, and the kids learn a lot. Talk to Lisa Grantley about it." He took the papers out of our hands and slid them into the dry side of the case, then gave Ivy a second look. "Weren't you already interviewing her?"

"Yes," Ivy said. "We're interested in a teacher's perspective."

"You're at school an hour early to talk to me about middle school politics?"

"What do you mean?" She consulted her watch. "It's twenty after eight."

Mr. Vannick's mouth dropped open, and he looked at his own watch. He shook his wrist. "Are you kidding me?" he shouted.

In a flash all of the ruined papers and his sopping wet coat had been stuffed back inside the broken briefcase. He hugged it shut and hustled up the sidewalk into the school.

"C'mon," I said to Ivy. "Let's go deal with our client."

... .- -- -..-. ... .--. .- -.. .

Meredith pounced as soon as we entered the office. "Did she tell you?" she demanded.

I nodded and dropped into my chair. "There's a new rumor floating around."

"It's careening around, smashing my future to bits." Tears pooled in her eyes, and she swiped at them hastily.

"Whatever they're saying, it's not the end of the world." My attempt at comfort was met with angry glares from both Meredith and Delia.

"They're saying that Lisa is going to formally ask Meredith to step down at the meeting." Delia whispered as though speaking below full volume would make it less true.

"People are saying she has *proof* that I'm incompetent," Meredith said, a sour note coloring her voice.

That was interesting. "Proof," I said as Ivy and I exchanged a sidelong glance. "As in, she has the checks?"

"I have no idea," Meredith said. "But I did find this in my locker this morning." She handed me a folded piece of paper. This one read, *You were warned. You didn't listen. Prepare for your CONSEQUENCES.*

Pacing back and forth, Delia squeezed her hands together nervously. "This is getting really serious, guys. Don't you think it's time to go to Mr. Vannick?"

"No," I said firmly.

Delia shook her head, prepared to argue the point.

"He's a suspect," I said. Delia's jaw dropped in shock, and even Meredith looked a little stunned. "After investigating Bradley and Lisa all week, we suspect they're not working alone. Who else would have something to gain from the student council being disbanded?"

"Someone who resents the time spent staying late," Ivy piped up, catching on to my train of thought.

"Someone who's a strong enough leader to convince them to do something illegal," I said.

Meredith sank down onto the guest bucket and buried her

face in her hands. "That makes sense, actually." Her muffled voice came through her fingers. "I can see Bradley and Lisa doing his dirty work."

"No," Delia burst out. "That's crazy. He's a teacher."

"That just gives him a title to hide behind," Ivy said.

"Delia," I said. "We were hired to figure out who's behind this. Trust us to do our job." I clapped my hands together to bring us back on point. "The good news is—I have a plan. Meredith, when have you usually been receiving the notes?"

"Sometimes before, but usually at the end of school."

I nodded, taking note of that schedule. Everything depended on successful timing.

"Your plan had better work, Howard." As she calmed down, Meredith reverted to her usual state of snippiness. "Pull the plug on these rumors, and find those checks. I'm over this." She stalked off, the guest bucket toppling in her wake.

Delia rushed over to right it and offered a small, apologetic smile. "She's not usually like this, you know."

Ivy looked like she was about to burst out laughing, and I motioned for her to zip it.

"She's not," Delia said, eager to defend her friend. "It's stressful being treasurer. And it means a lot to her. This whole thing with Lisa and Bradley has made it worse."

"That's no excuse for how she treats you," Ivy said. "Why are you even friends with her?"

Delia fixed her attention on dusting dirt off the bucket. "She used to be different," she said at last. "I have to ride out this craziness, and when things go back to normal, we'll be back to having fun together. I know it." Delia picked up her bag and rubbed a hand against her neck. "I'll see you guys later."

Ivy waited until Delia had turned the corner of the shed before bounding up to the desk.

"What's the deal, partner?"

"We're going to trace the rumors to their source, then stake out Meredith's locker and catch the blackmailer in the act."

Ivy pursed her lips. "It's not the best plan I've ever heard," she said.

"Rule number six, Ivy," I said. "A bad plan is better than no plan."

"If you say so."

I hauled up my bag and led the way out of the office. "Let's roll," I said. "It's time to gossip."

Chapter Sixteen

The field of gossip in a middle school is a twisting, tangled landscape of truth, lies, and all the gray in between. Wading into the murk, Ivy and I interviewed kid after kid. With such a juicy mess on their plates, everyone was more than happy to chew over the details.

We met up before lunch to compare notes. Ivy had a pile of interesting tidbits to share.

"This kid heard that Lisa's going to call an assembly and fire Meredith in front of the whole school."

"Who'd you get that from?" I asked.

She scanned her pages. "A sixth grader who heard it from another kid named Scotty."

"Harris?"

"Yeah, you know him?"

I nodded. "Let's check it out."

We entered the cafeteria and made our way over to the music kids' table. "Howard!" Scotty called out as soon as he spotted me. He jumped up from the table and clapped a hand on my shoulder. "Guys," he said as I struggled to keep my balance. "This is the guy I was telling you about. He's awesome." I gave a little wave to the kids at the table who eyed me without interest.

"Hey, Scotty," I said, keeping my voice low. "I need a favor."

He bent his head. "Anything."

"You know what people are saying about Meredith Reddy?"

"Oh, yeah, I heard that Lisa's—"

"I know all that." I cut him off before he could get himself wound up. "What I need to know is who you heard it from."

His face sank like I'd asked him to give me his favorite puppy. "Can you ask for a different favor?"

"No, I can't," I said. "I won't tell them you told me, but I need to know."

"You're not going to like it."

"Hit me."

Scotty rubbed at his chin and looked away. "I heard it from a guy on my basketball team." He mumbled a name.

I didn't have time for this. It wasn't like I was asking him to divulge national secrets. I swallowed a growl of frustration. "I need a name, Scotty."

Blowing out a breath, he directed the words at my feet. "Miles Fletcher."

I slammed my notebook shut and stuffed it back in my pocket.

"I said you wouldn't like it," Scotty said, his voice small and quiet.

"Thanks, Scotty," I patted him on the arm. "Appreciate the help."

I strode away from the table, and Ivy loped after me.

"Miles Fletcher," she said. "Isn't he—"

"Yes," I said.

"So, now we have to talk to—"

"Yup."

"Okay, then."

I marched across the cafeteria, my coat streaming out behind me. I had to do this quick and without hesitation, like yanking off a bandage. Heads turned as I walked by, but I didn't stop— didn't even look to make sure Ivy was behind me. I knew she would be.

Miles was at a table with a pile of his jock buddies, all of them laughing and throwing food at each other like primates. I stepped up to the table. After a quick double take, Miles relaxed back into studiously ignoring my existence.

"I need to talk to you," I said, loud enough for my voice to carry over the racket.

He lowered his eyebrows and shook his head slightly. The other kids at the table fell silent. Some stared; the rest smirked.

I took a deep breath. "Miles, I need to talk to you. It's serious."

He finally looked at me. "Oh, well, if it's serious." He turned back to his gang of morons, and they yukked it up.

Bellying up to the table, Ivy stuck a finger in his gut. "Listen, you," she said. "We've got questions, and we can ask 'em here or in private. One way will be more embarrassing than the other, and you've got two seconds to decide which one it'll be."

Miles waved her off, and Ivy said, "One . . ."

"Get lost," he said.

Ivy leaned in until she was nose to nose with Miles. "Two," she whispered and reached into her pocket. She pulled out a piece of paper and flashed it in Miles' face. He glanced at it and stiffened.

"Okay," he stood up, "I'll answer your stupid questions."

We led him out of the cafeteria, away from big ears and curious minds. Once we turned the corner, Miles stopped and leaned against the wall with his arms crossed. "That's far enough," he said. "Let's get this over with."

"You passed on a rumor to Scotty Harris about Meredith Reddy getting the boot," I said, pacing the floor in front of him.

"Yeah, so?"

"Who'd you hear it from?" I faced Miles, forcing myself to look him in the eye.

"Lots of people." Miles studied the wall, tapping the floor with the toe of his shoe. "Everyone's talking about it."

"Who'd you hear it from first?" Ivy asked. She came to stand shoulder to shoulder with me.

Miles paused his sulking long enough to look down at Ivy. "Lisa's best friend," he said. "If that's not a legit source, I don't know what is."

"Bradley Chen?" I asked.

"That's what I just said."

I waved a hand at Ivy. "Let's go."

Miles scoffed. "Typical."

"What?" I wheeled back to face him, resentment burning a hole in my stomach.

He straightened up from the wall and took a step toward me. "How about 'thanks, Miles,' 'appreciate the help, Miles.'"

And I thought his opinion of himself couldn't get any higher. I grabbed his hand for a shake. "Thanks, Miles," I said. "Appreciate you helping to spread nasty rumors, Miles." I dropped his hand. "Not that I expect anything less."

He looked sideways at Ivy. "You friends with this guy?"

"We're partners," Ivy said.

"Good luck with that. Remember not to try anything new without his permission," Miles said, sneering at me as he started back to the caf. "He doesn't react well to change."

"See ya, Miles," I said to his back.

Waving a hand over his head, he pushed open the door. "Later, Howard."

I looked over at Ivy and pointed at her watch. "What time is it?"

"Howard." She stood there, hands on her hips. The flicker of sympathy in her eyes had me cursing Miles all over again.

I threw my arms out, shaking off the past. "What?"

"Oh, please," Ivy said. "What was that? Miles?" She waved her hands in the air. "The weirdness?"

I groaned. Ivy was determined to hash through old history, like I hadn't bled enough for one day. "I already told you," I said. "He ditched me and Noah when he leveled up on the school food chain. End of story."

"Sounds like there's a little more to it than that." My new partner was nothing if not tenacious. "Care to shed some light on his words of warning?" she asked.

"No."

Ivy grabbed me by the sleeves and gave them a yank. "Howard, talk to me," she said. "If we're going to be partners, I need to know the truth."

The words "junior partner" were barely out of my mouth before Ivy let out a small scream of frustration. "Howard, you tell me the whole story right now or I swear I'm walking away."

"Fine," I said, wrenching my arms out of her grasp. "You want to know? Here it is. Yes, I didn't like it when he first started joining teams." I paced in front of the lockers, annoyed at myself for getting so worked up. Nothing like talking to Miles to make me lose my cool. The talking had been unavoidable, but letting him get to me wasn't. I knew better.

"Sports were never our thing," I explained. "We were more superhero costumes and card games. When he started hanging out with those meatheads, I couldn't see how we fit anymore." Pointing a finger at Ivy, I stopped. "But you know what he left out? How very quickly he proved me right."

Ivy had opened the door, and my pent-up grievances came out in a tidal wave. "He and his *friends* stuffed my head in a toilet after gym. They tried to hang me from the bleachers by my shorts after school. One of his new idiot buds almost broke Noah's nose playing dodgeball. They—"

Ivy held her hands up. "Howard, it's okay. I get it."

"*It's okay?* I'm glad I have your permission to be upset about this."

"No, I mean . . ." Ivy sighed and slid to the floor, "I know how hard it can be when someone abandons you like that."

I kicked at a bottom locker and then gave it one more for good measure. "What would you know about it?"

"My mom left," Ivy said. "Back in January. That's why my dad moved us here. I wasn't handling it well."

Nothing throws a sucker punch quite like perspective. I plopped down on the floor beside Ivy, taking a moment to absorb that newsflash. "Define not handling it well."

"Oh, you know," she said breezily, "joined every club and team there was to keep busy. My dad and I went to counseling. None of that helped, so I got creative. Tried my hand at shoplifting and other stupider stuff."

"I knew I should have asked for a background check."

Ivy rolled her eyes, but at least it got a little smile out of her. "I got caught before I did any serious damage," she said. "But it was enough to earn me a one-way ticket to the merry old land of Grantleyville."

"The punishment does not fit the crime in this case," I said. "Sorry about your luck."

"It's not as bad as I thought," she said. "You're a pain, but Miles seems like a real sweetheart."

I couldn't hide a grimace. "Too soon."

"I take back the Miles bit, but you're still a pain."

"Good enough." I rested my head against the lockers. It was a funny thing, thinking you had someone pegged, only to find out there was a whole different story below the surface. I looked over at Ivy. "Do you talk to her?"

"My mom?" Ivy shook her head. "A phone call here and there. Nothing that counts."

"That's the first conversation I've had with Miles since last May," I said. "One chat every six months is more than enough."

We sat there in woeful silence. I had no idea what else to say.

"At least we know each other's deep, dark issues now." Ivy laughed weakly.

"Are you okay?" I coughed and fumbled for my words. "About your mom? Are you okay now?"

"Are you okay about Miles?"

Fair point. "While we're discussing His Jerkness, what'd you use to get him to talk?" I asked Ivy.

She pulled out a piece of paper from her pocket and showed it to me wordlessly. It was one of the photos of me, Miles, and Noah from the home office. We were dressed up in homemade superhero costumes for Halloween a few years ago. Goofy grins stretched across our faces. Any fight that was left in me seeped out as humiliation took its place. I didn't know which was worse—that my ex-best friend was embarrassed to talk to me or that he was more embarrassed by proof we used to hang out.

"Why do you even have that?" I moved to grab the photo from Ivy, but she stuffed it back in her pocket before I could make contact.

"I thought I should get started building my own files," she said.

It was a good practice to get into. Except. "Does that mean you're starting a file on me?"

"Seemed like the thing to do," Ivy said with a shrug.

I had one on her at home, so I couldn't really argue. In fact, I should've been pleased about what an effective teacher I was. Temporary junior detectives—they grow up so fast.

"Okay," I said. Time to get this case back on track. "Let's get out of here."

She pushed her hair back from her face. "What's next?"

"If the blackmailer keeps to schedule," I said, "Meredith should be getting a letter by the end of school. I think it's time for a stakeout."

Ivy grinned. "My favorite."

Chapter Seventeen

The bell rang, and Ivy and I snuck down the hallway to our stakeout spot. Ivy had her own ideas about how the plan should play out.

"It'll be fine, Howard," she said. "Let me run this one by myself, and you'll have more time to work on other stuff."

"No way," I said. "You've never done a stakeout before. I'm not leaving you on your own."

"Uh, excuse me." Ivy stopped in her tracks and set her hands on her hips. "I was on a stakeout three days ago."

"Crashing one doesn't count. No more buts," I said. "Either we do the stakeout together or you don't do it at all." I was still in charge, and letting a junior partner run a major operation like this just didn't fly.

Ivy scrunched her nose as she thought about it. "Fine."

The best spot to see Meredith's locker was from Pete's supply closet. Earlier, I'd promised him an extra pack of jellies so he'd leave it unlocked for us. I held open the door for Ivy, and we slipped inside.

The closet was poorly lit and stank of industrial-strength cleaner. Ivy looked around at the mops and brooms hanging from the wall and scowled. "I can't decide if this is a step up or a step down from the girls' bathroom."

I scrubbed at a mysterious substance on the floor with my foot. "It's a lateral move." Kneeling down, I checked the sight line from the grate to Meredith's locker. A bit of an angle, but it would work. The hallway was deserted since most kids didn't stick around after school. No blackmailer was going to sneak past us.

Ivy flipped over a garbage bin and sat down, legs splayed out in front of her. "So, exactly how much of your time would you say is spent lurking behind doors, spying on people?"

"Paid or unpaid?" I asked.

Her laughter trailed off when she realized it was a serious question. "Um, I guess both. Although that's—"

"Shh." I waved a hand at her and held a finger to my lips. "I hear someone."

She jumped up and started toward the door when I stopped her with my foot. "No, stay back," I whispered. "They're coming this way." I rolled to the side and flattened myself against the wall. Ivy and I held our breath as the footsteps approached the closet.

The steps stopped right in front of the door, and for a moment nobody moved.

A key rattled in the lock.

I had seconds to come up with a plan. Whoever was coming through that door could ruin everything. Ivy was staring, waiting for me to make a move. There was nowhere to hide. I needed a reasonable explanation for why we were in the closet. Panic began to crawl up my chest.

The key turned, and I dove at the door.

Apparently, holding it shut was my best plan. I braced my hands against the sturdy wood, prepared for the worst, when the lock clicked into place. I may have underestimated what the worst could be. Yanking on the handle told me what I already knew. We were locked in. I dropped down and pressed my face against the grate to get a glimpse down the hall. A sharp pain tore through my leg as Ivy scrambled over me to try to get a look for herself. "Did someone just lock us in here?" she asked. "Did you see who it was?"

"No," I said. "Whoever it was had enough brains to stay close to the wall when they walked away."

"Hey," Ivy called out. "Hey, we're locked in here!"

"Can it." I poked her in the ribs. "Anyone catches us, we'll be suspended."

She poked me back. Hard. "We wouldn't be in this mess if you'd let me do the stakeout on my own."

"Oh, really?" I snorted.

"Yup." Ivy flopped against the wall. "Even if I got locked in, you'd still be on the outside to set me free."

"Take your twisted logic and put it to better use," I said. "We need to figure a way out of here."

"You're going to have to give me more responsibility at some point," she grumbled.

"Ivy, give it a rest. We've been partners for four days." The longest four days of my life.

She sat bolt upright and held up a hand. "I hear footsteps," she said. "Maybe they're coming back."

Ivy flipped over onto her stomach and joined me to peer through the grate. We heard the voices before we saw their owners.

"It's Bradley and Lisa," I whispered. Maybe this stakeout wasn't going as badly as I thought.

"And then, worst of all," Lisa said as they came into view, "I find out she's not even a reporter for the blog. It was a big fat lie!"

Bradley nodded. "She's a pretty good actress. I'm actually glad she came out to Drama Club."

Ivy grinned widely at me with both thumbs up.

"Focus, Bradley," Lisa snapped. "They're becoming a serious problem."

"I am focused." Bradley stopped in the middle of the hallway, right in front of our door. Ivy and I held perfectly still as he pouted. "You need to relax," he said. "There's a plan, remember?"

Lisa took a deep breath and let it out, closing her eyes and opening them with new resolve. "Right. Okay," she said. "Let's go find out what the rest of that plan is."

They walked down the hallway, out of sight, and we heard the door to the outside open and close.

"We have to get out of here," I said, leaping up from the door. "We've got to follow them and find out who they're meeting."

Ivy scrambled up beside me and nodded, zeroing in on the task at hand. "Okay, inventory. What do we have?" She examined the shelves and piles of stuff hanging from the walls.

"Broom, mop, mop bucket—" I tuned her out as I began my own furious brainstorm.

The lock mechanism was only on the outer knob so there was no way to pick it. We could break the handle on the door, try to remove the bolts, or take out the grate. Not enough tools and not enough time for any of those plans. We needed something simple. Something we could do right now. A ladder hanging in the corner caught my eye.

"Ivy, quick, rule number three. What's next door to us?"

"One of the girls' bathrooms," she said, a wary look on her face. "Why?"

"I have a plan."

I grabbed the ladder and set it in the middle of the closet. It took up nearly the entire room but it fit. I climbed to the top and popped up a ceiling tile.

"Up and over," I said, grinning down at my partner. "Problem solved."

"Nope," she shook her head vigorously. "Not gonna happen."

"Toss me my bag," I said. She hurled it up at me. I caught it and managed to stay on the ladder. This plan was coming along nicely. I set the bag on the top step and started pulling off my coat. "We don't have a lot of options here, Ivy. I'll go first and all you have to do is follow."

"Because that's gone incredibly well for me so far."

I stuffed my coat into my bag before slinging it over my shoulder. "You can come with me, or you can wait until Pete gets back in the morning to let you out."

Ivy gave the sleepover idea serious consideration. I didn't have time to wait for her decision. Someone had to catch up with our perps. "All right, see ya," I said as I climbed to the highest step on the ladder.

"I'm coming, I'm coming," Ivy groaned.

I slid the ceiling tile off to the side and levered myself up onto a metal beam. For once, I was grateful to be small. It was cramped and dark up there, laced with cobwebs and dust.

"I cannot believe I'm doing this." Ivy's head poked through the hole in the ceiling, and she glowered at me on my precarious perch. "If we die, I'm gonna kill you."

"It's ten feet," I said. "Stop being a baby."

Ten feet that took us about ten years to cross. Inch by inch, Ivy and I crept along the beam. We travelled in silence, too intent on our task to both talk *and* keep a careful eye out for the spiders whose homes were draped across our backs.

Bright light peeked through a crack in one of the tiles below. I stopped, and Ivy's head bumped into my butt. "Are we there yet?" she asked.

"Actually, I think we might be." I reached down and gingerly tugged the tile out of place. Hanging onto the beam for dear life, I leaned down as far as I could to look into the bathroom. The coast was clear. Our open patch of ceiling was over the last stall. I grabbed hold of the beam and lowered myself through the opening until my feet touched the top of the partition.

That was as far as I got.

"Howard," Ivy whispered. "Why aren't you moving?"

"I'm trying to figure out how to get down." All the reasons why Pops and I put the tree house at ground level came rushing back to me.

"I thought you had a plan," Ivy said as she scrabbled forward on the beam. Squinting at me through the dim light of the ceiling, she assessed the situation. "Why don't you let go?"

"Ivy, I'm balancing on a piece of metal that's about two inches wide. If I let go, I'm gonna fall into the toilet."

"I have an idea."

"I'm all ears."

"Give me your bag," she said. I worked it off my shoulders and carefully passed it up to her while keeping one hand firmly gripped on the beam. Ivy lay flat with her legs wrapped around the supports. She held my bag in two hands, the straps hanging down toward me. "Hang onto this," she said, "and lean down until you can grab the top of the stall."

"How is that going to help?" I asked.

"If you fall, you've got the bag to hang on to."

"Rule number six," I reminded myself. It was a terrible idea, but I didn't have anything to offer in its place. I moved my feet so they rested sideways on the cubicle wall and then looped one arm through the straps of my bag. Taking a deep breath, I very slowly and carefully began to lean down over the divider.

"Howard, we don't have all day," Ivy said, giving the bag a little shake.

I froze in place, resisting the urge to snarl at her in case the vibrations shook me off my ledge. "One tug on this bag and I'm taking you down with me, sister." On a shaky breath, I reached the last few inches and placed a hand on top of the stall. Once again I was stuck, with one hand slung over my head and the other resting on a section of metal I was sure hadn't been cleaned since it was built. This was the worst game of Twister in my life.

"Okay, Howard," Ivy said. "Unhook your arm, and swing down to the toilet."

I glanced up at her and back down into the cesspool I was

about to use as a life raft. "I can't wait until it's your turn to do this," I muttered.

I'd like to say that what happened next was a masterful display of fluid grace and cool athleticism. In reality, I did manage to unhook my arm and grab the top of the stall. At that point, I lost my balance and swung over the side, shrieking. My feet slipped and I clung to the partition while trying to find the top of the toilet with my feet. After a few desperate flails, my toes touched porcelain.

"How you doing there, buddy?" Ivy asked, her lips quivering with barely suppressed laughter.

"Piece of cake," I said and patted the metal wall in front of me. "Especially since now it's your turn."

She grinned at me before tossing my bag down onto the floor. It sailed through the air, landing with a splat.

"I could have taken that." I eyed my poor, abused bag lying half-open on its side. Even money she owed me a new apple.

"You're too busy watching the master at work," Ivy said.

"I thought you hated this plan," I said.

"Now that I've seen you do it, I know what mistakes to avoid." She swung herself down and balanced her feet on the wall. Keeping two hands on the beam, she carefully walked along the edge to the front of the stall. "Six years of gymnastics, finally making themselves useful." She reached down, gripped the top of the door and vaulted onto it, riding high as it swung outward. "C'mon, Howard Wallace," Ivy called as she leapt off the door and stumbled across the floor.

I gingerly stepped off the toilet and made my way out of the source of my future nightmares. Ivy stood proudly in the middle of the room, covered in dust and cobwebs. She burst out laughing. "Oh my gosh," she gasped. "You should see yourself right now."

"Come on, enough goofing around," I said. "We can still catch Bradley and Lisa."

"Wait, wait, wait," Ivy said. "Howard. We just *crawled through the ceiling*. That's some super-mega-professional P.I. stuff right there. Let's take a moment to celebrate."

She made a good point. I'd never pulled off something that impressive before, and Ivy had helped, in her own nearly-dumping-me-in-a-toilet way. A small celebration was probably in order. I held up my hand. "High fives?"

Ivy yanked up my other hand and slapped them both with her own. "Double high fives. Go team!" She smacked my hands a few more times, and we grinned at each other like idiots until—

"Uh, Ivy."

"I'm still celebrating."

"Okay, but—"

"Still celebrating."

"Is that spider in your hair celebrating too?"

Ivy shrieked and started swatting at herself wildly. She heard my chuckle and shot eye-daggers at me.

"Not funny, Howard."

"Sorry," I said. "I'll get it." I scooped the spider out of Ivy's hair and passed her a pile of paper towels. "Let's get cleaned up and get out of here." She let loose one last flail and then scrubbed at the cobwebs draped over her sleeve.

We burst into the hallway precisely when Mr. Vannick came through the outer doors. He spotted us and scowled. Holding the door, he gestured impatiently. "Out."

"Yes, sir!" Ivy and I hustled through the door. I snuck a quick look behind us. Mr. Vannick was standing in the doorway, watching to make sure we left.

"Kind of weird he's still here," I said to Ivy.

"And that he was coming in from outside, where Lisa and Bradley were headed."

I nodded my head and stopped to face Ivy. "Are you thinking what I'm thinking, partner?"

She cocked her head and smiled. "That our theory about

Mr. Vannick being the mastermind is turning out to be more than just a theory?"

"He could've gotten into the office to get the key to Pete's closet," I said, getting more excited about the possibility.

"Exactly," Ivy said. "And he would've heard from Bradley and Lisa that we were getting close."

"He probably thought he could catch us trapped in the closet and get us suspended." I scanned the yard. Lisa and Bradley were long gone, but Ivy and I had a new angle to work. "You know, I think we've almost got this case in the bag."

I headed toward the bike racks and caught sight of Blue, once again the last, lonely bike left on the lot. She was leaning unsteadily to one side, and I had to chuckle. Blue knew how to milk a pose.

"I'm coming, Blue," I said, smiling at Ivy. "A little waiting never hurt anyone." Blue responded by tilting further and I squinted for a better look. Something wasn't right. She was barely upright and had one handlebar flung over the rack. I sped up to a run. There was a screech. Blue lost the battle with gravity and crashed to the ground.

I was by her side in less than a second. Blue lay feebly on the dirty pavement, her back wheel spinning slowly from the impact. Her front end was still raised a few awkward inches off the ground, held there by the chain locked to the rack. "Hold on, girl, hold on." I fumbled for the key and struggled to fit it into the lock. My fingers were like sausages, and the key slipped from their clumsy grasp, clattering to the ground. I reached for it and froze.

An ugly slit marred the smooth side of her front wheel. I poked a finger into it. Straight through. Clean, cold and precise. Stepping back, I examined Blue's back wheel. Another slit, wider than the first.

I couldn't breathe. Blue had no air left, and she'd taken mine with her. I sank to the cement, patting her blindly. Something crinkled and fluttered to the ground.

"Howard," Ivy said quietly as she bent to pick it up. She handed me the crumpled piece of paper. Block printing. It could have been Ancient Greek for all the ability I had to understand it at that moment. I blinked my eyes and handed it back to her to read.

It was a simple line.

"CONSEQUENCES FOR ALL."

Chapter Eighteen

I t was a long and painful walk home. Blue staggered back and forth on the sidewalk. I'd have carried her but it took all my strength to keep her upright.

Ivy darted along beside us. "Howard, let me help."

"This is my fault, Ivy," I said. "My bike. I won't pass her off on someone else."

I trudged along, one foot after the other, and tried to block out the dull sound of Blue's flat wheels on the cement. My stomach felt like it was filled with lead. I tried talking to keep her moving, repeating the same words: "It's okay, girl. I got you. It's okay."

Finally, my house loomed into view. "Want me to stay?" Ivy asked. "I'll call my Grandma, and I can stay."

"No," I said. "There's nothing for you to do."

"We're going to figure out who did this, Howard. They won't get away with it." Ivy touched one of Blue's handlebars. "Are you sure I can't help?"

"I'm sure." I met her gaze. "But thanks."

I dragged Blue up the sidewalk and into the garage, setting her upside down in her parking space. Best to take the pressure off her wounded wheels. Sagging against the wall, I slid to the floor. *Idiot. Stupid, stupid idiot.* My fingers clenched, and my nails dug into my palms. Someone trashed my office, and how did I react? Did I carefully investigate? Keep an eye on my loved ones? I banged my fists against the floor, feeling the need to pummel something. No, I ran around needling suspects like I was Sam freaking Spade. I thought I was brilliantly forcing the perp out into the open. Putting the pressure on while they made mistakes. I screwed up, but it was Big Blue who'd paid the price. I'd ignored rule number seven: never underestimate your opponent.

Stroking Blue's fender, I murmured apologies. It was never the private eye who got knocked down; it was always his best friend. I'd missed the boat on proceeding with caution. Time to get my act together and come up with a plan of attack.

The garage door rattled open, and its rusty squeals

startled me out of my revenge fantasies. My old man pulled in, brow knit at the sight of Blue and me slumped in our corner. He got out of his car and ambled over. "Blue, Howard," he said. "Lurking in the garage for any particular reason?"

I nodded my head to my prostrate partner. "Blue needs new tires."

He frowned and peered at Blue. "What happened?"

"We ran over a rock."

He took a step forward for a closer look. "A sharp, knife-shaped rock happened to pierce both of Blue's tires. Through the sides?"

"Yes."

He sighed and took his glasses off to rub his eyes. "Howard, what's going on? Has your P.I. thing gotten you into something dangerous?"

"It's nothing. It was my own fault. I wasn't paying attention." I boosted myself up from the floor and dusted off my bag.

He patted Blue's frame gently. "She's been a good old bike."

"She still is," I said, cutting off the eulogy. "She just needs new tires. I've got money saved, I can buy them myself."

Pops nodded. "We can go on Saturday." He turned abruptly to face me. "Howard, we haven't been spending as much time together now that you're back in school. I hope you know you can talk to me if you need to."

"It was a rock, Pops." I headed to the door. "Everything's fine."

Everything was a train wreck, but I wasn't about to tell him that. What should have been a simple case had turned into a personal attack. I couldn't let that slide. I wouldn't. Telling my old man about it would only put him in the way of what needed to be done.

Not revenge.

Justice.

I had the whole night to plan how to solve this case and make Lisa, Bradley, and Mr. Vannick pay.

Chapter Nineteen

The next day the sun was shining and the sky was clear. I half expected bluebirds to swoop through my window to help me dress. The weather clearly had no regard for the blackness of my mood. I threw on a pair of shades and slunk down the stairs. My mother stood in the kitchen packing up her lunch for the day.

I slid onto a chair and grunted. "Coffee, black."

She set a glass in front of me. "Orange juice. From the carton."

Nudging my sunglasses down the bridge of my nose with a single finger, I peered at her over the frame. "Orange juice is a mood enhancer. I require all of my surliness today."

The glass of juice was pushed closer. Its sunshiney contents sloshed around, mocking me with orange cheer. "Take it and thank me," she said.

I lifted the glass and tipped it in her direction before taking a gulp. "Thank you, Mother."

She leaned on the table and cupped a hand under my chin. "Try not to worry about Blue today," she said. "You and your father will fix her up this weekend, and she'll be good as new."

Big Blue hadn't been good as new since 1987, but I appreciated the sentiment and offered a weak smile.

"Need a ride to school?" she asked, ruffling my hair.

"No thanks," I said, ducking away. A walk would help me clear my head.

I plodded down the sidewalk. Fresh waves of grief for Blue washed over me. My feet were unaccustomed to the slap of hard cement against their soles. I stopped at the bottom of Maple Street and glared at the hill stretched out before me. It was going to be a long walk.

Today was make it or break it for Meredith's case. My plan was risky, but it was the only way to catch our blackmailer. I hoped Ivy would be on board. If she wasn't, I was on my own. No place I hadn't been before.

A shadow spread across my path and stopped me cold.

"Morning, Howie." The banes of my morning commute stood an inch in front of me. Normally, I could endure Tim and Carl as a mildly amusing inconvenience. Today, I wasn't in the mood for subpar banter and amateur strong-arming. A sidestep around Tim was met with an implacable hand on my chest.

"Please. Don't," I said.

"Where's your lady cycle today?" Tim asked. He stood there, stroking his two pathetic strands of facial hair, and cold resentment flared in my gut. Big Blue had received enough abuse at the hands of miscreants; I wasn't about to allow these morons to jump on the pile. Tim rolled back on his heels, and a snarky smirk twitched his lips. "Is she home, cleaning up her rust spots? Or did you finally put her out of her misery and take her to the dump?"

Rage blazed inside me, intensifying as I thought of Bradley, Lisa, and everyone else who'd jerked around me and Blue this week.

This year.

I was sick of being smart. Sick of being a pushover. Blood pounded in my ears, and all I could see was Tim's face, cackling at his own cut-rate jokes.

A sharp snap cracked through the air. In the silence that

followed, Tim looked shocked. He raised a hand to his cheek, and Carl frowned. I stared at my own hand in disbelief.

"You're going to regret that, Howie," Tim said. His face went white, my red handprint vivid against his cheek. "I'm going to kill you dead!"

A number of thoughts ran though my brain in rapid succession while my insides turned cold. I was shocked I'd actually struck Tim but even more surprised that a slap turned out to be my go-to move. It was a new level of old school for me.

"I'm going to tell my father, and he'll destroy you!" Tim was still ranting. "And then I'll kill you again!"

"Tim." One word from Carl had us both stopping in our tracks. "Calm down."

"Carl, this kid attacked me, and you're telling me to *calm down*?" The rest of the red was returning to Tim's face.

I inched away, hoping to use the distraction for a quick getaway. Carl reached out and snagged my collar in one lightning-quick move.

"You're going to tell your dad that you couldn't deal with this little twerp?" He shook me once for emphasis. "You want that getting around school?"

Tim's look of confusion must have mirrored my own. I

couldn't tell if Carl was getting me out of trouble or making it worse. Apparently neither could Tim.

"What are you saying? We let this aggression stand?"

"Be the bigger man," Carl said. I was filled with sudden love for Carl. "Teach him a lesson, and let him go on his way," he concluded.

Wait, what?

Tim approached, cracking his knuckles, as I stood frozen in place. I had no backup and no escape. This was not going to be pretty.

"Hang on," I said.

My tormentors stopped and stared.

"Is the W toll still an option?"

"Shut up, Howie." Tim sneered and lunged.

Chapter Twenty

My cheek throbbed as I hobbled to school. Tim subscribed wholeheartedly to the "eye for an eye" philosophy. Or slap for a slap, in this case. Other than that, I wasn't much worse for wear. He'd roughed me up a bit, but his heart wasn't really in it. It would take him a while to get over the shock of me taking a stand. I wasn't proud of it. Well, a little bit proud. But violence was not the ultimate solution to the Tim and Carl problem.

"Howard!"

Ivy was waiting for me at the corner by the school with Meredith and Delia a step behind. She looked me over with a raised eyebrow. "What the heck happened to you?"

"A poorly timed moment of lightning-fast reflexes."

"Couldn't have been that fast."

"It started out well."

"And ended with your face like that," Ivy said. "You need practice."

"Not planning on it anytime soon." I nodded at the girls behind her. "To what do I owe the welcoming committee?"

Ivy passed me an envelope. "This." The piece of paper inside was wrapped around a small rectangle. I unfolded it to reveal a check stub and a note that said "*Say goodbye to the activity fund.*" Enough was enough.

Meredith was abnormally quiet, her face drawn and sad. All the fight had drained out of her. "It's over, Howard," she said. "They've won. I'm going to the principal's office to tell Mrs. Rodriguez everything."

Delia nodded and wrapped a supportive arm around her friend's shoulders. "It's for the best. She'll know how to make things right."

I pulled up the collar of my coat and stepped toward Meredith. "You're forgetting one important piece of information," I said.

"What's that?" Meredith eyed me with trepidation.

"I have a plan."

"You said that yesterday."

"This is a better plan."

Meredith and Delia started to protest, and I cut them off with one quiet statement.

"They attacked my bike."

The girls fell silent, and I let that sink in. I sat heavily on the bike rack and ran a hand along Blue's empty space. "They sliced her up and left her on the ground," I said. "I'm not walking away from that."

Meredith came and sat beside me. "Okay."

"What?" Delia squawked, and Meredith shushed her.

"Howard's had that bike forever," Meredith said. "That was a rotten thing for someone to do."

"I feel bad for you, Howard, but this is ridiculous," Delia said. "Over a silly bike?"

"Blue's part of the team," Ivy said. "She deserves justice." I met Ivy's eyes, and she smiled. "We'll get them."

"If you have a plan," Meredith nodded, "I say finish it."

Delia shook her head. "This is a mistake," she said. "There's Mr. Vannick. Let's settle this now." She waved wildly as the man himself came whistling up the sidewalk. "Mr. Vannick!"

He waved back. A flash of gold glinted in the sun. "Good morning!" he said. "How is everyone today?"

The girls answered in a chorus of goods and fines while I crept closer to Mr. Vannick. That flash had been a fancy new wristwatch. My eyes darted to his other hand. It held a smooth, brown leather briefcase.

"That is a fine-looking bag, sir. Is it new?"

"Why, yes!" he said, beaming with pleasure. "I got it last night."

No wonder Mr. Vannick was in a good mood. He was having a field day parading around with his ill-gotten gains. Concern creased his forehead as he surveyed the schoolyard. "Where's your blue cruiser today?"

I stiffened. "Why do you ask?"

"It looked like a neat old bike. It'd be a shame to hear you had to retire your wheels." He chuckled like he'd made a joke. Nobody laughed.

"My bike's at home," I said. "She's taking a personal day."

Our eyes locked, and I caught an odd flicker in the depths of Mr. Vannick's. He held up his wrist. "Look at the time. I've got to head in. Nice talking to you, kids." Mr. Vannick slid his gaze away and hurried up the sidewalk into the school. Lisa and Bradley appeared at the entrance and waved him over. He stopped to talk, all three of them glancing back to look at us.

"Do you believe me now?" I asked Delia.

"That was kind of bizarre," she admitted.

"Do what you have to do, Howard," Meredith said.

I grabbed Ivy's arm. "We're going to go prepare."

"What's this great new plan?" Ivy asked as we walked away.

"We search Mr. Vannick's classroom and find the checks."

Ivy choked and coughed until she found her voice again. "What?"

"It's the only way I can think of to get hard proof," I said. "You don't have to come. If we get caught, it'll be serious. I can do this myself."

"Are you kidding? I've been waiting all week for something like this," Ivy said. "Don't you dare leave me behind." Reaching into her bag, Ivy pulled out her own pack of Juicy. "Just tell me when and where."

Chapter Twenty-One

We had to wait until lunch to carry out our plan. Mr. Vannick was in the teachers' lounge, and the coast was clear. Ivy played lookout while I tested the door to his classroom. Unlocked. We dashed inside, and the door closed behind us with a quiet click.

"I'll take the desk," I said. "You check through the closet."

"This is more like it," Ivy said. She rubbed her hands together with gleeful relish. "We're finally doing some real detective work."

"What are you talking about?"

"Aside from getting locked in a closet, all we've done is talk to people and spy on them. It's about time we did some decent digging."

"That *is* real detective work," I said. "Ninety percent boring and then ten percent borderline criminal."

Ivy laughed. "What do you mean 'borderline'? Two minutes ago we broke into a teacher's classroom."

"Technically, no, we didn't. It wasn't locked." I opened a desk drawer. "And neither is this, so we're good."

Opening the closet door, Ivy stepped inside. "*Blergh!* Organize much, Mr. Vannick?"

"Start with his coat and briefcase," I said. "We have to find something to tie him to the blackmail." I started to comb through the desk and kept one eye on the door. There hadn't been enough time to nail down Mr. Vannick's schedule, so I had no idea how long our window of opportunity would last.

There was a framed picture off to the side of a smiling brunette and two small girls. I assumed they were his wife and kids. Judging by the happy expressions, none of them were aware he was a cold-blooded bike-mangler. I flipped the picture down. I needed to focus on the task at hand.

The top drawer held a stash of vanilla mint gum. Any doubts I'd had about the man's character were solidified right then and there. No checks or half-written blackmail notes, though. "Find anything yet?" I asked Ivy.

Her muffled voice floated around the closet door. "*Nada.*"

We hadn't searched thoroughly enough. Mr. Vannick was behind this. I was sure of it. Once we had our proof, he would pay, and he could start with Blue's physical therapy bills.

I opened the third drawer and shook my head. Birthday cards. They were probably covering up the checks. I picked them up and looked down. The bottom of the drawer was filled with office supplies and stickers. My heart did a slow turn in my chest. I opened the first card: *Happy Birthday, sweetheart. Try not to get coffee on this one.* The swirly handwriting was followed by a dozen *x*'s and *o*'s. My mouth went completely dry. The next card was filled with drawings and childish scrawl. I peered at the scribbles for a closer examination. It looked like a stick-figure man with a watch around his waist. I scanned the desk and spotted a small calendar. There was a tiny cake doodled on yesterday's date.

"Ivy," I said. "I've made a very large mistake."

"What?" she called out, stepping out of the closet.

The doorknob rattled. A male voice drifted in: "Wait a minute. I've got to grab my coat."

"Rule number nine," I said to Ivy. Shoving her back in the closet, I grabbed Mr. Vannick's coat before I shut the door. Just because I was breaking rules left, right, and center didn't mean Ivy had to. I dropped the cards into the drawer. Mr. Vannick walked in the room and stopped abruptly when he saw me standing there. I used the awkward pause to surreptitiously close the drawer with my foot.

"Your coat, sir?"

"What are you doing in here?" Mr. Vannick strode over to the desk and spotted the other three drawers that I hadn't yet managed to close. He snatched his coat out of my hands and pointed at the door. "Office. Now." He took a quick look around before he propelled me out of the room and pulled the door shut behind him.

We were halfway down the hall when I heard the soft click of the door again. Ivy had made it out. Rule number nine: don't get caught. At least I still had someone on the outside.

Maybe she could swing my bail money.

Chapter Twenty-Two

My parents and I sat huddled in the principal's office. Ms. Kowalski was there too, as my homeroom teacher, but also, I was pretty sure, for her own amusement. She kept fidgeting in her chair as little bubbles of glee fizzed through her. Bearing witness to me being hauled before the principal was probably the highlight of her teaching career. The air was thick with silence and the dry scent of pencil shavings. I didn't realize anyone used pencils anymore, let alone pencils that needed to be sharpened. Maybe it was a special air freshener sold to principals to add a subliminal sense of academia to their workspace.

Pops and my mother were seated on either side of me. They bent back in their chairs to hold a silent conversation over my head, which involved them widening their eyes at each other at various intervals in between stares: a highly advanced form of parental Morse code.

Mrs. Rodriguez entered with Mr. Vannick, crowding six people into an office built for two. She sat at her desk and opened the file that lay on it. Mr. Vannick stood to the right of her desk, at ease, his arms crossed loosely and one foot propped against the table leg. An awkward silence stretched out while we waited for her to finish reading the details of my crimes. She paused midway to put on her glasses. It was a fairly hefty file.

"So, Howard Wallace," Mrs. Rodriguez said at last. "You broke into Mr. Vannick's office."

I raised my hand in protest. "That is inaccurate," I said.

"Pardon me?"

"Not your fault; you didn't have all the facts."

"Howard," my mother said, a warning hiss in her voice.

"What I meant was the door was unlocked, so I did not, technically, break in."

Ms. Kowalski smiled. She loved it when I tried to argue my way out of things. My attempts usually started out strong, but quickly spiraled toward detention.

In this instance, the point needed to be made. It was a key argument in my defense.

"Fine," Mrs. Rodriguez said. "You entered Mr. Vannick's classroom and began to search through his desk—"

"Also unlocked," I said.

Five pairs of eyes bore into me with varying degrees of hostility.

"Please continue," I said.

"Thank you," she said with a gracious nod. I couldn't tell if there was any underlying sarcasm in the move. Mrs. Rodriguez was good.

"Howard, please tell us why you were searching Mr. Vannick's desk."

There was only time for a split-second decision. Truth or lie? A lie wouldn't fly with this crowd. Not when the eyewitness was standing in the room. I decided to go with a truth bomb.

"I was looking for evidence," I said. "Because Mr. Vannick was a suspect in a case I'm working."

"What case?"

"I can't tell you that without breaking detective-client privilege."

"That's not a thing," Mr. Vannick said, rolling his eyes with a snort.

I leveled a steely glare at him. "It is if you want to stay in business."

Mrs. Rodriguez cleared her throat and closed the file. "I'd like to speak to Howard alone for a few minutes."

Ms. Kowalski grumbled as my old man touched my shoulder. "That okay with you, bud?" he asked. I nodded, and they all filed out of the room. The door closed behind them, followed by a brisk flurry of chair squeaks. Probably Mr. Vannick and Ms. Kowalski fighting over the best eavesdropping spot.

Mrs. Rodriguez pressed her palms together and watched me over her steepled fingertips. I returned the gaze with a cool one of my own. Rule number eight: never tip your hand.

"I want you to tell me the whole story," she said. "From start to finish. And then we'll see how I can help you solve this situation you're in."

"Principal-student privilege?"

"Within reason."

Any delusions I had about how this chat was going to go vanished instantly. "Within reason" was the phrase adults used when they wanted a back-door exit on a deal. Mrs. Rodriguez didn't care about my reasons. In her eyes, I was guilty, and she was just looking for more dirt to add to the pile. This cozy chat was a fishing expedition in disguise.

We'd see about that.

"Why don't we start with who hired you, Howard?"

"I'm sorry, ma'am," I said. "To divulge that information would betray my client's trust."

The ticking of the wall clock filled the silence as Mrs. Rodriguez studied me. "What was your case? I need *some* sort of information to work with."

I chose my words carefully. "Blackmail."

"What kind of blackmail could you have possibly thought Mr. Vannick was involved in?" She sat back in her chair in bewilderment.

"The threat-filled kind," I said. It was as detailed as I was willing to get.

Mrs. Rodriguez leaned forward and tapped a finger on my file. "Howard, I don't think you're taking this situation seriously."

"With all due respect," I said. "I wouldn't have entered that classroom unless I was serious."

"Were you working alone?"

"Yes."

"Do you have anything to say in your defense?"

I'd said all I could without dragging Ivy or Meredith into it. Keeping them clear was the best I could hope for at this point. If I could ride this mess out, I might be able to keep the whole case from circling the drain.

"Howard?" Mrs. Rodriguez was watching me, waiting.

"No, ma'am," I said. "There's nothing else."

"Very well," she said, disappointment skirting the edge of her tone. She stood up and walked around her desk to the door. "I need to speak with your parents, and then we'll discuss your punishment." The door clicked shut behind her.

Right. Punishment. That was to be expected, I guess. No matter. I could take my lumps same as the next guy. I passed the time by inspecting the framed degrees and certificates hanging on the wall. They looked impressive—exactly what the home office needed to spruce it up a bit.

The door opened, and the adults funneled back in. My parents resumed their seats on either side of me. They each placed a hand over mine, and the faith I had in weathering the storm began to falter. I wondered how severe my punishment was going to be.

"Howard," Mrs. Rodriguez said. "I admire your ingenuity and dedication; however, your methods leave something to be desired. First, I would like you to apologize to Mr. Vannick."

I stood and faced Mr. Vannick. "I apologize for misreading the evidence that you seemed to present," I said. "I made a mistake and acted rashly. I promise never to do that again." His forehead puckered in concentration, and I turned to Mrs.

Rodriguez before he could pinpoint the holes in that apology. "You said 'first.' What's next?"

"You're suspended for the rest of the day," she said. "Starting Monday, you will undergo an in-school detention for the next three weeks. Mr. Vannick will decide what tasks you'll complete during that period."

That cleared up any lingering pout on his face. Mrs. Rodriguez wasn't finished. "Lastly, there is to be no more private detective work conducted on school grounds. Your 'office' will be dismantled. That is my final word on the subject."

I kicked myself for not thinking of that possibility. It was going to seriously cut into my productivity, but I could make it work. The business would survive. My parents thanked Mrs. Rodriguez and ushered me out of the office.

We were halfway to the parking lot when I spotted Pete demolishing my corner. He'd cleared away the three-legged desk and stacked the pickle buckets neatly to one side. I jogged over before my parents could tell me to stop.

"Pete."

"Howard." He nodded glumly as I walked up. Pete was going to miss his weekly six-pack nearly as much as I was going to miss the office. "This is rotten luck," he said. "But it was good while it lasted."

"Do me a favor, Pete?" I kept my voice low. "Don't get rid of this stuff."

Pete scratched at his chin and kept one eye on my approaching parents. "I don't know, Howard," he said. "The boss said to take it all to the dump."

"Have a little faith, would you? I'm down, but I'm not out."

He kicked at one of the buckets. "You're pretty out."

My mother was almost in earshot. The time for haggling was gone. "I'll keep paying rent if you store it for me," I said.

"Deal." Pete nodded as a hand clamped down on my shoulder.

"Time to go, Howard," Pops said.

My parents hustled me into the car before I had a chance to shake on it with Pete. As I sat down, I suddenly realized Ivy had no idea what was going on. My partner was in the wind, and who knew where I was going to end up?

I'd messed this case up royally. I followed the rules, and all of my plans went down the tubes. Now the blackmailer had the upper hand. If I didn't turn things around, the bad guys were going to win, and my P.I. business wouldn't be worth the sticky notes it was written on.

Chapter Twenty–Three

As Pops pulled into our driveway, my mother twisted in her seat to look at me. "Go inside, Howard," she said. "And go to your room."

Unbuckling my seatbelt, I headed into the house. Once my coat was hung up and bag dispatched on the floor, I went up the stairs to my room and shut the door. I waited a couple of minutes before creeping out onto the landing. I wasn't an idiot. They were obviously going to discuss phase two of my punishment, and I needed all the information I could get before I mounted my counterargument.

The acoustics in the hallway were not ideal. I shimmied forward to the top step. Better, but not perfect.

Snatches of conversation volleyed up the stairs. I could

hear enough to know the discussion had morphed into a fight. My mother said they'd "played along long enough" and I "didn't live in reality." My work took me to the seedy underbelly of Grantleyville Middle School. If that wasn't reality, I didn't know what was.

The back door slammed: Eileen was home. I heard her walk toward the living room, but she detoured for the stairs, redirected by the sounds of our parents' argument. Spotting me on the top step, she grimaced.

"I'm assuming this is your fault."

"I could make a case for it being Mr. Vannick's," I said.

She joined me at my post and ground a knuckle into my shoulder. "What did you do?" she asked.

"Got picked up doing a little B&E for a client."

"Ugh," she said. "Mom and Dad had better ground you good this time. You get away with murder around here."

I scrubbed a hand over my face and huffed out a breath. "They're deciding my fate as we speak."

"I don't know why I'm the only one who thought this was inevitable," Eileen said. "Maybe this will get it through your head. You're a kid, Howard, not a detective."

"Artistflower461," I said.

"Excuse me?" Eileen went still.

"The password for your computer. Don't tell me I'm not a private detective." Her face went white and then a very interesting shade of red.

"Oh, and I added Michael Anjemi's cell phone number to your contacts list since you love him so much."

"You. Are. The. Worst." Eileen grabbed my head and stuffed it down between my knees before she stomped off to her room . . . presumably to change her password, not that it mattered.

I was the worst. I was the best. It all depended on your perspective.

I returned to my listening and was met with silence. I dove back into my room, not a minute too late. "Howard," Pops called from the bottom of the stairs. "Please come down here."

Taking my time going down the stairs, I ran through the possibilities. A grounding for sure—the folks couldn't let a suspension go unanswered. No TV—I could live with that. Probably yard work; Pops hated it and passed it off at any opportunity. Sitting through a lecture was a given.

My parents sat on the couch in the living room. Fixing on my very best remorseful look, I hopped on to the loveseat facing them.

"Howard," my mother said. "What happened today was

very serious. Your father and I have discussed what further action needs to be taken here at home."

Pops cleared his throat. "And what we've decided, your mother and I, is that you are no longer to do investigative work of any kind."

I froze as shock rocketed through me. "You're joking."

"No, Howard," my mother said. "We're very serious. Your behavior has been unacceptable."

Ignoring her, I turned to my father: Brutus Wallace. "You love my investigations. We talk about my cases all the time."

He sighed. "I encouraged you when I believed it was a healthy outlet. You were so miserable this summer, with Noah moving and Miles—"

"Stop bringing him into it." This was all excuses and double-talk. I thought my father knew that being a P.I. was more than a means to an end.

"We were happy to see you actively interested in something."

"And now you want to take that away." I couldn't even look him in the eye. I swallowed down hard on the bile rising in my throat. They had no idea what they were doing to me.

"You behaved in a completely inappropriate and disrespectful manner today," my mother said. "You have lost the right to be out playing detective."

"I never played," I snapped. "And I didn't do anything Philip Marlowe wouldn't have done."

"Howard." My father's sharp tone made me jerk in my seat. "*Philip Marlowe* is not real. You are not in a story. Your actions have consequences."

"I know that"—better than either of them.

"You're almost thirteen. Today you behaved like an irresponsible child. You've given us no choice but to treat you like one."

My mother reached beside her and pulled something brown on to her lap.

My coat.

"We're getting rid of this," she said and sniffed. "After I wash it."

"So, that's it. No discussion. No negotiation." The rank taste of betrayal filled my mouth. Of all people, I thought my father understood my work. Understood me.

"You didn't give us any choice, Howard," he said. "You went straight to breaking and entering."

"It *wasn't locked.*"

"The fact that you're still arguing that point proves we've made the right choice," he said. Right choice for them. From my end, it was six shades of wrong.

"Where was Ivy during all of this?" my mother asked. "Should we be calling her parents?"

Ivy. The last thing she needed was more black marks on her record. Her father brought her to Grantleyville for a fresh start, and I'd provided a detour. So far, I'd managed to keep her out of hot water. If my parents bought my song and dance, maybe she could keep her new beginning.

"No," I said. "Ivy had nothing to do with it. I already told Mrs. Rodriguez, I did this by myself."

My mother was primed for further interrogation when my father gently set one hand over hers. "We'll take your word for it," he said. "Go back up to your room. We'll call you for dinner."

I took the stairs up at a snail's pace. No use expending energy on speed. I had nowhere to be. The last few hours felt like a terrible chapter out of someone else's life. One wrong turn had destroyed everything.

The phone rang, and my father picked it up. "Oh, hello, Ivy," he said. I paused on the step.

"No, he can't come to the phone right now. He's grounded. Yes, you can call tomorrow. Maybe he'll earn time off for good behavior. Bye-bye." He hung up the phone and waved me upstairs. My stomach lurched. Now I had to figure out how to tell my partner she was out of a job.

Chapter Twenty-Four

Saturday marked the beginning of my forced retirement, and I'd yet to wrap my head around being plunged into a life of leisure. Fortunately, my father seemed determined to help me fill up the hours. We spent the morning changing Blue's tires, and I took her for a few loops in the driveway. She started out a bit rocky, but bounced back to her good old clangy self quickly enough. It was nice to see her on the mend. At least one of us was back on track.

I gave Blue a quick wash and shine, trying to shake the sinking feeling growing in the pit of my stomach. Ivy still had to be filled in on the new law of the land. I could only imagine how well that was going to go over. I'd rather sit through the lecture from my parents again.

Blue's handlebars swung to the right as I polished off her back fender.

"What? You want to chime in on this mess too?"

She hit me with a pointed look.

"Fine," I said. "I'll call her." Grumbling about bossy know-it-all bikes, I thumped inside and picked up the phone. Taking a deep breath, I dialed Ivy's number.

"What is going on?" she demanded, answering on the first ring.

"Hi, Ivy," I said.

"Don't you 'hi' me; tell me what's happening. Why is the office gone? What did Mrs. Rodriguez say? Meredith is freaking out, but I think I talked her down for now."

I told her the whole story and ended with my parents' ban on P.I. work. She raged over the injustice of it all, and I waited for her to wind down.

"Okay, what do we do now?" she asked.

"Nothing," I said. "Wallace Investigations is kaput. All cases are closed, solved or otherwise."

"I repeat, what do we do now?"

"What do you mean?"

"Are you allowed visitors? Should I bake a cake with a file in it?"

Relief flooded through me as I caught on. I suddenly realized I'd half-expected her to ditch me once the P.I. biz was out of the picture.

Lucky for both of us, my mother felt a ban on detective work was ample punishment and, given her concerns about my socialization, barring my only friend was out of the question. I'd been given strict instructions on what to say when I called Ivy. "You want to come over tomorrow? Watch a movie?"

"Works for me," Ivy said.

... .- -- -..-. ... .--. .- -.. .

She showed up at two the next afternoon. After a single knock on the back door, she let herself in and toed her shoes off onto the mat.

"Make yourself at home," I said as I walked into the kitchen. "Person who's never been in my house before."

"Don't be rude to your only friend," Ivy said.

"Follow me, friend." I led her into the living room, and she flopped down on the couch.

"Ooh, snack mix." She reached out and grabbed a handful from the bowl on the table. Joining her on the couch, I started the movie my father had set up for us to watch. Something about alien robot machine things. We watched it in silence for about five minutes before Ivy sat up abruptly.

"What IS this?"

"Alien robot machine things," I said. "The sequel."

She shook her head and scrambled up on to the arm of the couch. "This is ridiculous."

I crunched on a couple cheese puffs and contemplated the giant action figures pulverizing each other on the screen. "I agree," I said, "but I think there're some good explosions later on."

"No, this!" Ivy waved her arms at me and the couch. "This is ridiculous. I can't believe we're actually watching a movie."

I reached over to grab the remote and pressed Pause. This conversation had somehow taken a left turn, and I needed to focus. "But that's why you're here."

"No. No," Ivy said as she bounced over from her perch to kneel beside me on the couch. "I'm here because I thought 'watch a movie'"—she lowered her voice to a conspiratorial whisper—"was code for 'break me out of house arrest so we can finish investigating this case and catch the jerk who sliced up Big Blue.'"

My stomach dropped as Ivy's words hit me. "Wow," I said, blinking under her intense stare. "You read a lot of code into 'come over and watch a movie.'"

This conversation was headed into dangerous territory,

and I no longer had a lucky coat. I latched on to the next best defense: avoidance.

I grabbed the remote and pressed Play. The crashing clang of metal on metal filled the room. Ivy snatched the remote from my hand, pressed the Power button, and tossed it behind the couch. We stared at each other in silence before she poked me in the shoulder. Hard.

"Howard, come on," she said. "Talk to me. Don't you want to finish this thing?"

"There's nothing to finish, Ivy." I picked up the bowl of snack mix and dug around for a pretzel. "Wallace Investigations is dead. We killed it."

"You're being dramatic."

Passing the snacks over, I looked her in the eye. "I'm telling you the truth. It's over. Rule number ten, remember?"

Ivy sat up straight and shoved the bowl back into my lap. "Exactly," she said.

This could not be good.

"Pick your battles, Howard." Standing, she set her hands on her hips. "How could I forget?"

I set the bowl on the table. "Ivy—"

She cut me off with a finger wag. "Pick your battles," she said again. "It doesn't mean you don't fight if you can't win. It means you fight for what matters. Fight for what you love." Ivy slammed a fist into her hand, punctuating her point with a determined smile. Obviously some sort of response was required.

"Are you thirsty?" I asked. "I think there's some juice in the kitchen."

She groaned. "Howard, work with me here. You can't just roll over on this." Her eyes narrowed. "Right," she said, clapping her hands together sharply. Ivy pivoted on the spot and stepped up onto the coffee table. I sucked in a breath. My mother would kill us both if that thing got scuffed. Ivy paced back and forth, kicking the snack bowl out of her way as she went.

"Quit it," I said as pretzels and cheese puffs went flying across the floor. "You're never going to be allowed over again."

"Don't care," Ivy said. "We have more important things to deal with." She stopped pacing. "Are you going to tell me that the guy who broke into a teacher's classroom—"

"It wasn't locked."

"*Still talking!*" Ivy held up a finger. "Are you going to tell me that the guy who searched a teacher's classroom, stared down a Grantley, and survived being locked in the janitor's closet doesn't love being a P.I.?"

I stayed silent. Ivy could rant all she wanted; it wouldn't change the situation. She was pushing me into an impossible spot. If I did any more investigating, my parents would ground me for the rest of my life—or worse. As much as I hated giving it up, there was no other choice.

Ivy obviously didn't see it that way. She resumed her pacing on the poor, abused coffee table.

"Are you going to tell me that the guy who built his own office out of scraps and pickle buckets is willing to let it all fade away?"

I stared at the TV and tried to will it to turn back on.

"Are you telling me"—Ivy stuck her hands on her hips— "that the guy who interrogated his evil ex-best friend is too scared to get back out there?"

"Ivy, stop." The plea popped out before I had a chance to catch it.

"Howard, what are you so scared of?" She hopped off the table and sat back on the couch. "Getting caught again? Because I don't care about that."

I fought against the torrent of words that threatened to erupt from my mouth.

"I do," I said.

Ivy scoffed, doubt clear in her eyes.

"Seriously think about it," I said. "We go investigate, get caught, then what?"

She jerked her head toward my plainclothes T-shirt and jeans. "They already took away your coat and your office. What have you got to lose?"

Everything I'd lost too many times before. Everything I was scared I'd never have again. A big question with a simple answer—what have I got to lose?

"You."

Ivy opened and closed her mouth once, frowning. "Howard—"

"I get in trouble again, they'll ban you, and I'll be back at square one."

"A big weirdo whose closest friend is a cranky thirty-five-year-old bicycle?" Ivy bumped her shoulder against mine.

"As delightful as Blue is, friendship with her has its limits," I said with a thin smile.

We sat in silence for a moment before Ivy shook her head. "You're being ridiculous, you know that?"

The phrase "talking to a brick wall" suddenly came into my mind. "Ivy, I'm trying to save our friendship here."

"I'm trying to save *you*," she retorted.

"Oh, please."

"How long do you think you'll be able to keep up the regular kid act?" she asked. "Two weeks and you'll go crazy.

Then you'll be miserable and we'll still end up not friends because you'll be unfit for human company."

"I like the odds of my plan better than yours," I said. "I'm not willing to risk it."

"I thought we were partners," Ivy snapped. "Don't I get a say in our future? Don't I get a vote?"

"Ivy."

"You're not the only one who's had a miserable year," she said. "You're not the only one who's been sad and angry and needed something *more*." Tears threatened to spill over, and Ivy swiped at them furiously. "This meant something to me too."

"I'm sorry," I said. I'd never felt like such a spineless worm. My stomach began to curl in on itself, and I pressed a hand to it. "I can't do what you want me to do."

"I'm not asking you to do it alone."

"It's too much, Ivy," I said. "For both of us."

"Exactly, Howard. This is bigger than just you or me. This is about principles." Ivy dropped her head against the back of the couch. "Detective work is your life. You love it. I love it." A small worry line creased her forehead. "If we don't fight for that, when is anything going to be worth fighting for?"

I let her words sink in, and the terrifying truth of them hit the center of the black ball of fear in my gut. Nothing had ever fit me as well as being a detective did. I'd been deceiving myself about how easy it would be to let it go. Ivy was right. If you don't fight when you have everything to lose, what you have isn't worth keeping.

For once, I had something worth keeping.

Ivy squinted at me from her side of the couch. "What's happening?" she said. "What's going on in there? Are you monologuing? I've learned to recognize the signs."

I sat bolt upright and slapped my hands down on my knees. "I've decided you're right." My heart pounded, and I didn't bother to curb the grin stretching across my face.

Executing a complicated seat dance, Ivy threw a fist in the air. "Yesssssss."

Our next few moves needed to be carefully planned out if we had any hope of avoiding disaster. In the history of my life choices, this one was going down as a doozy, but I'd be lying if I said it wasn't fun.

Ivy rubbed her hands together. "Plan. Lay it on me."

"Break me out of house arrest, to start," I said.

Her smile turned calculating. "Easy," she said. "We convince your mom to let you come over to my place for dinner. She loves me. She'll totally go for it."

"What are we actually doing?"

"Going to the Grantleyville Community Theater rehearsal. A little birdie told me that's where Bradley would be this weekend."

I scratched at my nose to hide my grin. "Was this birdie named Bradley?"

"You betcha. He invited me after the Drama Club meeting."

"Lucky girl."

"Okay, let's blow this popsicle stand!" Ivy jumped up and did a little boogie.

I grabbed her sleeve before she could charge out the door. There was such a thing as priorities. "First we have to clean up. My mother will hit the roof if she sees this mess."

Ivy shrugged, bending down to pick up a cheese puff. "Piece of cake." She blew on the puff and popped it in her mouth. "We'll be done in no time."

No time turned into quite a bit of time. Ivy'd managed to kick snack mix into every nook and cranny of the living room. When I was finally satisfied my mother wouldn't collapse at the sight of the place, I turned to leave and found our exit blocked. This mission was going to fail before we even made it outside.

My sister Eileen stood in the doorway surrounded by an air of smugness only a vengeful sibling could generate. "Going somewhere, Howard?"

Chapter Twenty-Five

"**W**hat do you want, Eileen? I'm a little busy at the moment."

My sister pushed off the door frame. "What do I want?" She chuckled—never a good sign. "No," she said. "This is about what you want. And what it's worth to you."

Ivy and I exchanged uneasy glances. "Don't know what you mean," I said.

"I heard everything. I know what you're up to," she said. "I could go and tell Mom right now."

"Were you listening in on our conversation?" Ivy stalked up to my sister, propelled by her outrage. I put a hand on her shoulder to pull her back and got a dirty look for my trouble.

"No," Eileen said. "That's Howard's usual method. Word to

the wise, Ivy: next time you give a rallying speech—talk quietly."
She looked at me. "You're lucky the parents are outside."

I racked my brain trying to figure out what to do and
leapt on the first idea that came to mind. "Tell on me and
I'll disclose that your study session at the library last week was
actually a party at Tammy's house."

Eileen threw up her hands. "This is what I'm talking
about. I can't do anything without you sticking your nose in
it," she said. "There is a thing called privacy, Howard." She
opened her mouth to yell at me some more but then shook her
head. "You know what? I don't care. Go ahead and tattle. It'll
be worth it to see you get nailed for trying to bust out." Eileen
turned to leave, and panic overrode every other thought I had.
Ivy and I were finishing this case. We couldn't be tripped up
before we even left the house, especially not by my evil sister.

"Wait," I blurted out.

She stopped in the doorway, not facing us, but not leaving
either. Progress.

"What's it going to take?"

She looked over her shoulder at me. "For my silence or my
help?"

"Both."

That reeled her in. Eileen sauntered back into the living

room. "It's a pretty big thing you're asking," she said as she picked up a pretzel from the snack bowl and popped it in her mouth. I wasn't about to tell her where they'd been. She sat down on the table and settled the bowl into her lap.

"Ideally, my price would be you staying out of my business," she said. "But that would last less than a hot minute." Eileen tapped a pretzel against her chin. "My second choice is free detective services for life."

"That's ridiculous, and it's not happening," Ivy said, arms crossed.

They both looked at me, expecting an answer, and I took my time thinking one over. As far as I was concerned, this was more solid ground. Favors are a P.I.'s best currency.

I could negotiate.

"One case."

"Three cases, and you have to do all my chores for a month."

Ivy made a strangled noise in her throat as I considered Eileen's counteroffer. Three cases were a risky bet. Who knew what my devious sister would come up with?

"One case," I said. "And I'll do your chores for two months."

Eileen bobbed a nod and held out her hand to seal the deal. "Agreed."

We shook on it and got to work.

"Your first mistake," Eileen said, "is thinking you can charm your way out of the house. You're grounded, and any love Mom has for your little sidekick here isn't going to change that."

"I am offended by at least three parts of that statement." Ivy said. I silently pleaded with her to let it go. "But I'll survive," she continued. "Eileen, try a cheese puff. They're delicious."

Coming up with a plan was going to take longer than actually carrying it out. "What are you thinking, Eileen?"

"I could tell them you're sick," she said. "Keep them out of the living room until you got back."

"No dice," I said. "They'd want to check in on me and see what's wrong."

Ivy and I weighed our options on the couch while Eileen made her way through the tainted snack mix.

"I've got it." My partner snapped her fingers. "We tell them you're coming over to work on an extra-credit project."

My sister and I looked at each other and burst out laughing. "That would never fly," I said.

"The parents would be all over it," Eileen agreed.

"We could tell them you annoyed me," Ivy said. "And I locked you in your room." She smacked me in the shoulder.

"Ow." I rubbed at the spot and thought it over. "That might actually work."

The back door opened and closed as my folks entered the kitchen.

"Stay here," Eileen whispered. "I have a plan."

I held on to the hem of her shirt. "Share the plan."

"We need to play on their concerns about you, and, trust me, they have many," Eileen said, batting my hand away. "I'm going to go in there and soften them up. Let me work my magic."

I preferred to put my trust in a well-thought-out strategy over magic, but my sister was already out the door. She walked into the kitchen while Ivy and I crept along the hallway. By the time we got close enough to listen in, her pitch was underway.

"He needs to get out more, Mom," Eileen said.

"Well, he's punished," was my mother's patient reply.

My sister paused for full dramatic effect. "I saw him talking to his bike again this morning."

"Blue's been through a rough patch," my father chimed in. "She needs some extra TLC."

"Can we *not* with the whole 'the bike has feelings' thing?" Eileen sighed. "And you wonder why Howard is so weird."

There was another pause. I knew exactly which Look my mother was wearing. "That's enough, Eileen," she said. "I appreciate your concern, but we're dealing with your brother, and that's all you need to know."

"Fine," Eileen said. "Let him lose all his friends. Sorry. *Friend.*"

Ivy pointed at herself and grinned. *That's me,* she mouthed. I motioned for her to move back when I realized the silence meant my sister was coming our way.

Eileen stood in the doorway for her big finish. "At least I tried." She swirled out of the kitchen and whispered in my ear as she stalked by. "Seed planted. Give it a little bit before you go in."

We listened to my parents murmuring for as close to a full minute as I could make it with Ivy poking me in the side. After a brief, whispered argument, she agreed to stay in the hall while I took my turn at bat.

Conversation came to a halt when I slunk into the kitchen trying to look as pathetic as possible.

"Howard," my mother said. "Are you enjoying your movie?"

"Mov—yes," I said. I'd completely forgotten we'd been watching a movie. Sam Spade help me if she asked about the plot. "It's awesome, I love it, thank you for picking it." I heard a quiet thump from the hallway. The warning from Ivy was loud and clear: *Get to the point, Howard.*

"Ivy invited me over for supper," I said. "I know I'm grounded, and the answer's probably no." Cue a hopeful little smile. "But may I?"

My folks had one of their patented wordless discussions. I waited out the nods and eyebrow raises, milking that hopeful smile for every drop of sympathy I could.

"Okay," my mother finally said. "*But*, you go straight there. No side trips. No shenanigans."

I nodded, fingers crossed behind my back.

"Once you have dinner," my old man chimed in. "You come right back."

I opened my mouth to say "thank you" when Ivy bounded into the room.

"Great! Thanks, Mrs. Wallace," she said as she grabbed my arm. "Hi, Mr. Wallace."

My folks stared at Ivy and then me. They were on the edge of confused and teetering into suspicious.

"Come on, Howard, let's go." Ivy dragged me out the door as I waved good-bye.

Safely out on the driveway, I shook my head at Ivy. "Way to play it cool, partner."

"What can I say?" Ivy tossed back her hair. "I was born for the stage."

"And I know where to find you one," I said.

... .‾ ‾‾ ‾..‾. ... .‾‾. .‾ ‾.. . .. ‾‾‾ ‾. ...

The Grantleyville Community Theater troupe held their rehearsals at the senior center. Ivy and I strode through the entrance, full of a singular purpose—track down Bradley Chen. The apple-cheeked and cotton-haired receptionist brought us up short with a tiny, polite cough.

"Everyone needs to sign in, dears." She pushed a sheet of paper across the desk.

"Oh," I said. "Sure, no problem." I scribbled down a name and passed the paper over to Ivy.

"Rule number eleven," I whispered. When investigating, a good detective never leaves a trail.

"With a side of rule number four," she said with a nod. After finishing off her signature with a dot and a swirl, Ivy handed the sheet back to the receptionist.

I glanced at the nameplate on the desk and leaned over it with a smile. "Hazel—may I call you Hazel?"

She smiled back after squinting at the sign-in sheet. "Of course, Miles."

"My friend Lisa and I wanted to check out the theater group. Would you be able to point us in their direction?"

"Down the hall and to the right, the auditorium is at the very end there."

"Thank you, Hazel," I said, ushering Ivy down the hall.

"You're welcome, sweetie. Have fun." Hazel waved us off, and I used the brief window of time to review our plan of attack.

"We need to get him alone," I said. "We'll have better luck getting our answers without any witnesses."

"How are we gonna get him to talk?" Ivy danced down the hall, revving herself up like a boxer before a fight.

"Rule number twelve: everyone has a hook," I said. "You just have to figure out what it is in order to reel 'em in." We stood outside the auditorium and watched Bradley through a window in the door. He was running through the paces of a scene. "Got anything good on him?" I asked Ivy.

She nodded her head slowly. "I have something that might work. How do you want to play it?"

"Only one way springs to mind."

Her eyes opened wide. "Bad cop, bad cop?"

"How about you take the lead," I said with a grin. "I got your back."

"This is going to be awesome." Ivy straightened her shoulders. Serious business from head to toe, she pushed open the door and headed inside.

We stood on the sidelines waiting for Bradley to finish his scene. He caught sight of us near the end and fumbled his lines. So far, so good.

By the time we strolled up to him, Bradley had rallied his composure. "Hey, Ivy," he said. "Did you come to check out the group?" He flipped his hair out of his eyes and rocked back on his heels, cool as a cucumber.

Ivy whipped a notebook out of her pocket, and I felt a surge of pride. "We have more questions," she said.

"About Drama Club?" Bradley was either incredibly thick or a much better actor than I'd thought.

"No, Bradley," Ivy said. "About the trouble you and Lisa have gotten yourselves into. Blackmail's a nasty business."

A muscle in Bradley's jaw started to jerk. "I don't know what you're talking about."

"Why don't you step into our office," Ivy said, taking Bradley by the arm. I grabbed on to the other side, and together we hauled him out of the auditorium to the women's bathroom a few doors down.

Bradley brushed himself off and leaned against a sink. "Should I be calling my lawyer? I'm pretty sure this is harassment."

Ivy blocked the door while I checked the stalls. "So is sending someone threatening notes and vandalizing their office," she said. "Oh, but wait, you don't know anything about that, right, Bradley?"

He switched his gaze warily between me and Ivy. "Yes," he said. "That's what I'm saying."

"Let's talk about something else for a bit." Ivy tapped a pen against her notebook. "Drama Club was pretty interesting this week, don't you think?"

"Yeah, I guess."

"I liked the part when Mrs. Pamuk talked about how being on stage was a privilege, not a right." Ivy leaned in close. "If it came to light that someone was part of a cruel and illegal scheme, they'd forfeit that right, wouldn't they, Bradley?"

He pulled a pack of Juicy Smash from his pocket and fumbled out a piece. My memory teemed with images of my vandalized desk. "Mind if I take a look at that?" I asked, reaching for the pack.

"Yes. Why?" Bradley clutched the pack tighter in his sweaty palms. "No. Is this a trick?"

"It's just gum, Bradley," I cocked my head at him, "isn't it?"

He flipped the pack a few times and then handed it over. Popping out the gum sleeve, I looked inside the cardboard cover and nodded in grim satisfaction.

"You know, my office was broken into earlier this week," I said to Bradley as I passed the pack over to Ivy. "The only thing that was stolen was my Juicy Smash stock."

"What a shame," he said. "Why don't you have the rest of mine, since you've already taken it?"

"Actually, it *is* mine," I said. "See this here?" I pointed to the inside of the gum pack that Ivy held up for display. "I mark all my inventory. HW265. Howard Wallace, pack number 265."

Bradley gulped nervously, his eyes darting back and forth between me and Ivy. We had to dig in deep before he rabbited. Ever so slightly, I nodded at Ivy.

"That's some pretty serious evidence, Bradley," she said. "We take this to Mrs. Rodriguez and you're going to get detention for sure, maybe even suspended."

Swiping at the sweat on his upper lip, Bradley shook his head. "No. No, they said it would be fine. It's all going to work out fine."

"I don't know about that," Ivy said. "What do you think's going to happen once Mrs. Pamuk gets wind of this? The disappointment she's going to feel?" She clucked her tongue. "I think you'll be lucky if you make it onto the stage crew."

"Stage crew." Bradley wheezed out a breath and dropped his head down between his legs. "Stage crew. I can't breathe."

Ivy shot me a panicked look, and I motioned for her to keep going. She patted him on the back and bent down to speak into his ear.

"It doesn't have to be that way, Bradley. You tell us what we need to know, and we leave your name out of it."

Bradley's breathing began to slow, and his muffled voice drifted up. "No stage crew?"

"No stage crew, no suspension," Ivy crooned. "Nothing to stand between you and the spotlight."

After one deep sigh, Bradley straightened up and smoothed his hair back into place. He eyed Ivy for a long moment before—finally—his shoulders sagged in defeat and he leaned limply against the sink. "Okay, fine," he said. "What do you want to know?"

"Why'd you bust up my office?" I asked.

"It was part of the plan."

"The plan you and Lisa concocted to bump me off the case and get Meredith banned from the student council?" I stood elbow to elbow with Ivy, and we treated him to a couple of frosty stares.

"Yes," he said before shaking his head. "I mean no."

"Which one is it, Bradley?" Ivy asked.

"Give me a minute here, jeez." He began to pace and rub his stomach. Crime wasn't for everyone. "Yes, it was part of the plan but it wasn't *our* plan. She said if we stuck to it, everything would be fine."

"She?" Ivy demanded.

"You guys don't understand," Bradley whined. "We were really upset about Meredith getting elected, and everything she said made sense. It was supposed to be easy."

"We get it," I said. "You were hard done by; you were weak."

"You didn't know what you were getting into," Ivy chimed in. "Blah, blah, blah. Just tell us who 'she' is."

"I don't know," he said, tugging on his hair. "You don't know what she's like. No one does. She'll destroy me if I talk."

"Let's not exaggerate," I said.

"I'm not." Bradley shuddered. "She's scarier than Lisa."

I rolled my eyes at Ivy. Enough of this. We needed the ringleader's name, and we needed it now.

"Bradley. Stage crew," she said, holding up one hand and then the other, "or spotlight."

"Okay, okay, okay." Bradley stared at us and then laughed grimly. "I never wanted it to go this far in the first place. I only wanted to have fun with my friend."

"Give us the name." Pen in hand, Ivy had her notebook at the ready.

There, in our makeshift office at the Grantleyville Senior Center, Bradley Chen took a deep breath and spilled his guts.

Chapter Twenty-Six

Armed with all the dirty details, Ivy and I stood at the foot of a driveway only a few streets over from my own, staring up at the ringleader's house.

"Delia," Ivy said, still shaking her head. "I never would have pegged her for a stone-cold crook."

"She had us all fooled. The best criminals always do."

"Okay, but *Delia?*"

I scuffed at the driveway with my shoe. "What better way to stop a friend from ditching you than to destroy the thing they're ditching you for?"

The soft sounds of a quiet neighborhood drifted around us as Ivy thought that over.

"When you put it that way," she said. "I'm surprised the

basketball team is still standing."

The bark of laughter burst out before I could stop it. "Believe me, I thought about it."

"Well," Ivy said. "I, for one, am glad you decided to be the bigger man, relatively speaking—"

"Hey, now."

"—and go in a more interesting direction," she concluded.

"I'm glad you approve," I said as the front door to the house opened and a small blond boy emerged.

"Kevin?"

"Howard Wallace!" His face lit up as he ran over to us. "Did you find Spaceman Joe?"

"Not yet," I said. "Do you live here?"

"Yup," he said. "I have a little more money saved. Do you want a deposit?"

"Don't worry about it," I said, eyeing the house and the opportunity Kevin presented. "Is your sister home?"

Kevin scrunched up his nose and made a face. "No. What do you want her for, anyway?"

"I don't," I said. "You're just the man we came to see." Ivy shot me a look, and I grinned.

"What would you say if I said for one small favor, I'd consider your case paid in full?"

"For sure! Name it!"

Clapping a hand down on his shoulder, I busted out all the confidence and charm I could muster. Everything hinged on Kevin agreeing to this plan. "We need you to let us in to Delia's room," I said.

The little guy laughed in my face before cutting off abruptly. "Are you serious?"

"Are your parents home?" I started across the lawn to the house.

"My mom's in the backyard gardening," he said, scuttling after me.

"Excellent," I said and pointed at the front door. "Lead on, please, Kevin."

He looked back and forth between me and Ivy. I could see the wheels turning in his head as he processed the situation. "You want to investigate something in Delia's room?"

"Yes, Kevin."

"She's going to be pretty mad if I let you in there."

"Probably."

Kevin scratched at his nose while I resisted the urge to tap my foot. "Can I watch you work?" he asked.

I glanced over at Ivy, and she shrugged. "Sure," I said.

"Cool." He pushed open the front door and waved us

inside. "Her room's up here," he said, leading the way up the stairs.

"Did you take money from a little kid?" Ivy hissed at me as we reached the landing.

"No," I said. "Weren't you listening? We're on the barter system now."

"What is wrong with you?"

The price of doing business with Kevin became clear as he began a running commentary almost immediately. "This is awesome," he said. "I've never seen a real detective in action. Do you have a magnifying glass?"

I started to answer, but that didn't appear to be necessary.

"Are you working for the cops? Did an anonymous tip send you here? Are you going to dust for prints? Do you need to wear gloves? This is Delia's room." He pointed at a closed door to the left of us. "I have some winter gloves in my room. I'll go get them for you."

Ivy and I exchanged grins as Kevin ran off to his room. "After you," I said, bowing to my partner. She twisted the knob and opened the door.

"Wow," Ivy said. "Years from now, when people study this case, they'll say this is where she first went wrong."

We were adrift in a sea of pastel pinks and purples, frilly

bedspreads, and adorable cat posters. "Maybe gloves aren't such a bad idea," I said.

"Sorry, guys." Kevin burst through the door, pausing for a minute to catch his breath. "I couldn't find any."

"Don't worry about it," I said. "Just put yourself somewhere out of the way so we can get to work."

He scooted over to the bed and threw himself on top of it. Ivy and I poked around, opening drawers and combing through the contents.

"What did Delia do, anyway?" Kevin asked. "I mean, she did something, right? If you guys are here going through her stuff?"

"She made some bad choices," I said, taking a book off her desk to flip through. "We're here to help her make it right."

"I can help, if you want." He flopped onto his stomach and bent over the side of the bed to look underneath. "Kevin Potts, junior detective."

Ivy chuckled and shook her head. "Sounds like a plan, Kev. Let us know if you find anything."

I hoped he would, because we were coming up empty. Ivy and I'd rifled through all of Delia's drawers and shelves, turned her closet inside out, and scoured her entire desk. No checks. That was unacceptable.

No checks meant no case.

"Any luck, Howard?" Ivy's muffled voice came from behind the dresser.

"Nothing."

Taking one last turn around the room, I circled slowly, hoping something would pop out at me. A shelf I'd missed, a hidey-hole, maybe a big, flashing sign that said "Checks Hidden Here." We were running out of time.

The front door slammed. "Mom? Anybody home?"

Correction: make that out of time.

Kevin fell off the bed, his face ashen. "It's Delia."

"We gotta jet," Ivy said. "She can't find us here."

He blocked our exit and herded us back into the room. "Don't go downstairs. She's coming up, we need to hide."

"Where?" I looked around the ransacked room, which was getting smaller by the second. This was going to end in disaster.

Kevin stumbled over to the closet and opened the double doors. "Here, get in."

"I've hidden in more closets this week than I have my entire life," Ivy muttered.

"Kevin, you'd better not be in my room." Delia's voice rang down the hallway. "You know you're not allowed in there."

Ivy and I threw ourselves in the closet with Kevin close behind. I pulled the doors shut and pressed myself against the wall. Ivy was against the opposite side, and I could hear a slight rustle as she arranged the hanging clothes for camouflage.

Footsteps announced Delia's entrance followed by a muted shriek. "Kevin, why is my door open?" Something thumped as Delia walked into one of the piles on the floor. "What have you done to my stuff? Where are you? *Kevin!*"

He took a step backward, jostling a few hangers. We all froze. Very slowly, I turned my head and tried to get a glimpse of what was going on through the slats in the door. Delia whipped around and stared at the closet. Barely even breathing, I didn't dare move a muscle.

Our junior detective sneezed.

Delia leapt at the closet and threw open the door. She grabbed Kevin by the front of his shirt and hauled him out into the room. Sisterly rage clouded her vision. That and a surplus of winter clothes had allowed Ivy and me to escape detection. Delia only had eyes for poor Kevin.

"What are you up to?" She shook him once, and he held on to her arm for dear life.

"I was looking for Spaceman Joe," he mumbled.

"I told you he's not in here!" Delia flung out her arms,

shoving Kevin and sending him flying into her bedside table. Picture frames and knick-knacks spilled across the floor as he toppled over.

Ivy gasped quietly. I tried to make eye contact with her before she could do anything rash. Delia advanced on Kevin, and Ivy growled, wrenching back the door of the closet. "Delia, that is *enough*."

Not about to let my partner head out without backup, I scrambled out of the closet after Ivy and helped Kevin up off the floor.

Delia gaped at us, shock robbing her of full sentences. "Ivy? Howard? What are you—did you guys search my room?"

"Short answer—yes," I said.

"Why would you do this?" She waved a hand at the wreckage in her room. "Does Meredith know you're here?"

I kept my mouth shut, and Ivy did the same. Better to let Delia come to her own conclusions. Her eyes went wide, and she sank down to sit on the bed. "Am I a suspect?"

This was the Delia I recognized, not the one who'd freaked out on Kevin and had Bradley running scared. But just because it was familiar didn't mean it was the truth.

Tears filled her eyes. "Please," she said. "I don't understand. Will you tell me what's going on?"

Grabbing the desk chair, I sat facing our prime suspect. Two could play at this game. "Well," I said. "We had a lead."

"If you call Bradley blabbing everything a lead," Ivy piped up.

"I didn't want to get too technical about it," I said, propping my feet up on the bed. Delia's eyes darted from me to my feet to Ivy and back. "I guess you'd call it more of an overflowing confession of guilt than a lead."

"He started talking, and he wouldn't shut up." Ivy picked up a book from the floor and set it back on the shelf.

"Please don't touch my things," Delia said. "Howard, please don't put your shoes on my bed." I plopped my feet back on the floor, and she winced when a small clump of dirt rolled onto the carpet. "We always figured Bradley was involved, but what does that have to do with me?"

"You didn't make the best choice of partner-in-crime," I said. "He spilled the beans, right, Ivy?"

My partner was juggling a load of fairy statues and attempting to put them back on the desk. "Oh, yeah," she said. "Bradley cracked like a nut."

"Put those down," Delia snapped.

"What do you think I'm trying to do?" Ivy plunked the last statue down and dusted off a wing. "Where was I?"

"Bradley," I said. "Cracked like a nut."

"Yes." She snapped her fingers. "He sang like a bird."

"Squealed like a pig," I said.

"Popped like a zit—"

"Stop it!" Delia yelled. We were finally getting to her. "I am so sick of you two and your detective—"

"Language, Delia," Ivy said. "Not in front of the kid."

All three of us turned to look at Kevin lurking in the doorway. I'd almost forgotten he was there until things turned PG. "Did he spill like a glass of milk?" he asked, eyes wide.

"Get out of here, Kevin!" Delia leapt at the door and slammed it after Kevin fled into the hallway. She rounded on us, and the mask of Sweet Delia fell away completely. Her smile went sharp, and her eyes turned flinty. "So Bradley talked, and you think you know everything."

"Pretty much." I glanced over at Ivy, who nodded. I wasn't sure if this was progress or dangerous.

"You obviously don't have the checks," Delia said, strolling back toward the bed.

"We don't," I said. "But you do."

"What did I tell you about touching my things?" Delia shot a look at Ivy as she put a clock back on the side table.

"Just trying to help tidy up," Ivy said. She bent to pick up more stuff from the ground.

"You guys have already made a big enough mess. Stop making it worse." She paced around her room. "You're not getting anything out of me. You might as well leave."

"Delia, this is your friend we're talking about," I said. "Don't you want to do the right thing?"

"You don't get it, Howard," she said.

"Of course I do," I snorted. I probably understood better than anyone else at our school. If Delia wasn't so bent on total destruction, we could've had a bonding moment.

"That's right. I forgot about Miles," she said, sinking back into a frilly pink cushion. "You let him go pretty easy. Maybe you weren't such good friends."

Ivy scoffed from her corner. "Is that your measurement for friendship? The more you care, the harsher the punishment?"

"I'm not concerned with your opinions, Ivy," Delia said. "I'm speaking to Howard right now."

"It's none of your business," I said through gritted teeth. I needed to step up before I lost control of this conversation.

"Seems only fair since you're right in the middle of my business." Delia cocked her head to the side. "Does it still hurt? Being left behind?" She played with the ribbon on the bedspread. "I could help with that, you know."

Losing control had taken us to a very interesting place. "Do tell." I sat up in my chair, and Ivy watched us both from across the room. Delia smiled, pleased to have my full attention.

"Let this thing with Meredith play out," she said. "And I'll help you with Miles."

"How would you do that?"

"Howard." Ivy's voice was a low warning meant for my ears alone, but I couldn't help myself. I wanted to peek over the edge of the dark side and see what it had to offer.

"Tell me your plan."

Ivy groaned softly as Delia grinned. "Are you looking for reconciliation or retribution? I think door number two, in your case," she said. "There are a number of . . . creative ways to get someone kicked off a sports team. Or even better, get the team shut down all together."

"You seem pretty confident in your abilities."

"I've gotten this far, haven't I?"

"Delia, are you listening to yourself?" Ivy stomped over and stood between us. "Reality called. It misses you. It wants you to come back."

"Mock me all you want, Ivy," Delia said. "Howard understands."

I shook my head. "No, I don't, actually," I said, relieved to know it was true. There was a time when I might have thrown my lot in with Delia, but not anymore. "I think you're talking five types of crazy."

"True friends don't let *anything* come between them," Delia declared, slamming a fist down on the bedspread. The myriad of decorative pillows behind her were sent tumbling from their perfectly arranged pile.

"If you're really friends with someone, you deal with whatever comes between you," Ivy said. "If you can't, then maybe extracurriculars aren't the problem."

"Oh, be quiet, Ivy." Delia scrambled off the bed. "I didn't ask for your opinion."

In that moment, I felt nothing but pity for Delia. I'd been in her place. It was lonely and sad and full of confusion. But she'd still made a choice. A very deliberate one. "Do you think Meredith is going to want to be your friend once she finds outs out what you've done?"

"How's she going to find out? You have no proof."

"But we have a lot of questions." Ivy said.

"And when we start asking them," I said. "People will start connecting the dots."

Ivy stood beside me, arms crossed. "On a path that leads straight to you."

"Seriously. Stop it," Delia said with a laugh. "You guys are too cute. You're not going to say anything."

"How do you figure that one?"

"You start talking, I start talking," Delia said. "Your office at school was cleared out. Something tells me you're not supposed to be investigating anymore." She wagged a finger at me. I couldn't deny it, so I just glared.

"That's what I thought," she crowed. "And you definitely aren't supposed to be breaking into my house."

"Technically, Kevin let us in," I said.

Kevin's voice came muffled through the door. "That's true."

Delia let out a little scream and stalked up to the door. "Go *away*, Kevin." She gave it a good kick before looking back at us. "I think it's time for you to go."

"I think you're right." As much as I hated to back down from an interrogation, we weren't getting anywhere with Delia. It was better to retreat and regroup if we had any chance of coming up with a new game plan.

Delia escorted us to the front door with minimal gloating. Kevin was nowhere in sight. Smart lad.

"You shouldn't have come here today," she said as we made our way down the front steps. "Meredith's ready to drop the case. Everything was going to turn out fine."

"And now?" Ivy asked.

Delia stood in the doorway, steely-eyed and resolute. "Now you're a problem."

"Funny," I said. "I was thinking the same thing about you."

"The difference being that I like to make sure I take care of my problems," Delia said. "There are twelve hours until school tomorrow. Plenty of time to figure out how to dump this whole situation in your lap."

She slammed the door with a force that shook me down to my toes. Ivy and I were left in silence and failure. Mulling over everything we'd discovered, and more importantly, hadn't discovered, I sighed.

"I think that went well, don't you?"

Ivy burst out laughing, and I joined her. There wasn't much else we could do. Heading down the sidewalk, our laughter trailed off and reality set in.

"This is not good," I said. "I thought Friday was bad, but this is *bad.*"

"It does look dreadful," Ivy said.

"That was our last chance." I kicked at a mailbox as we walked by. "Now we have no proof against Delia, and she pretty much declared war on us."

"Yes," Ivy said, reaching into her pocket. "If only we had

some sort of evidence." She pulled out a rectangular package and tapped it against her chin. "That would have been helpful."

I stopped in my tracks. "What is that?"

"Oh, this?" Ivy grinned. "The checks."

"How?" I lifted them out of her grasp and held them up in awe. "Where? When?"

"All the classic detective questions."

"Ivy."

"Found them while I was tidying up Delia's stuff," Ivy said. "She was too busy yelling at you to notice."

I opened up the package and peered at the checks inside. "Where were they?"

"In the back of one of the picture frames that fell off the table." Ivy did a jazzy little celebration dance down the sidewalk. "It'd busted open a bit. The corner was peeking out, I spotted it and *voilà!*—checks."

It was official. I had the best partner ever. "I didn't even see you take them."

Ivy added some complicated hand moves to her dance. "I put my nimble shoplifting fingers to good use. Still got it!"

"I don't endorse stealing, but . . . good job!"

"So we got her!" Ivy held up her hand for a high five, and I frowned. We weren't in end-zone dance territory yet.

"Right, Howard? My hand is waiting."

"No," I said. "We have to clearly connect her with the checks." My brain was already working over every angle of this fresh glitch.

"I know that face," Ivy said. "That's your crazy-plan-making face."

"Crazy opponent calls for a crazy plan." I stuffed the checks into my pocket and high-fived Ivy's waiting hand.

"You heard the girl," I said. "We've got twelve hours before school tomorrow. Let's get to work."

Chapter Twenty-Seven

Monday morning came at its leisure despite my attempts to hurry it along. Ivy and I had plotted and schemed our little hearts out last night. I could only hope it would pay off. There was still one piece of the puzzle that had to fall into place.

By seven-thirty, I was in the garage, hauling Blue out to start her warm-ups. She was in high spirits, zipping around the driveway. New treads agreed with her. We had barely done a couple of turns before she darted down to the sidewalk, raring to go.

We traveled up to Maple Street. The sun was rising over the trees, and I could see Tim and Carl silhouetted at the top of the hill.

Waiting for me.

"Fingers crossed, Blue," I said. "It'd be a real shame if I got pulverized before seeing this through." We trucked up the hill to meet my possible doom.

"Got a lot of nerve coming back this way, Howie," Tim said as he stuck out his foot to stop Blue's front wheel.

Planting my feet on the sidewalk, I gave Blue a reassuring pat on her handlebars. "Not so much nerve as a lack of good sense," I said. "But why should we let that stop us, right, Tim?"

"I could knock some sense into you if you like." He took a step forward, cracking his knuckles.

"Not today, thanks," I said. "In fact, I have a proposition for you boys."

"A propo-what?"

"An offer," Carl said.

"A job offer, to be exact," I said.

"What's it pay?" Tim was a man of priorities.

"I'm getting to that," I said, holding up a hand.

Carl shot a sideways look at Tim. "That means it pays nothing."

"Let me explain." The odds of my face meeting the sidewalk were increasing the longer I stood here. I needed to make my pitch, and I needed to make it fast.

Tim and Carl rocked back on their heels, arms crossed, listening.

"You've heard rumblings about problems with the student council, yes?"

"Newbie member screwup," Tim said. "Lisa's been going nuts."

"Yes, good old cousin Lisa," I said. "She's in a bit of a pickle."

Tim looked pleased at that. The Grantleys were a close-knit and notoriously competitive family. I was counting on that working to my advantage.

"I'm closing in on solving this case," I said. "And I could use some extra muscle. That's where you come in." It was our genius brain wave last night: if you can't beat 'em, hire 'em.

I outlined my plan and what their role would be as hired goons. Tim and Carl stepped away to talk it over, but before you could say "Brute Squad," Tim was back.

He gripped Blue's handlebars and leaned in. "What would we get for our trouble?"

"A favor," I said.

Tim snorted.

"From Lisa." It was the ace up my sleeve and the only chance I had of this working.

"A favor from Lisa?" Tim's mouth dropped open and then snapped shut. "Miss 'Don't-talk-to-me-Tim-I'm-the-president' Lisa?"

"I don't think that's her exact title," I said. "But yes."

Carl moved into my line of sight, eyes narrowed as he watched the exchange between me and Tim. If I had to take a stab at the expression on his face, I'd say it was amused. Which was odd, but I had too many balls in the air to add puzzling out Carl to the list.

"I will take that deal," Tim said, offering his hand. We shook on it, and I gave them their final instructions before leaving.

Favors may be a P.I.'s best currency, but lies run a close second. Lisa would flip her lid over my promise of a favor to Tim. It was the only thing I could think of to get him to fall in line. She'd never agree to it, and then I'd be left holding the bag of debt to Tim. It was going to end in tears, most likely mine, but that was tomorrow's problem.

Today's were just beginning.

Chapter Twenty-Eight

I vy was already waiting at the school bike racks, locking up a scooter.

"Ivy, a scooter?"

"What?"

"I believe the rule is blend, not stick out like sore thumb."

"Says the guy with a bike three times older than he is."

I let that slide. Blue was in fine form for her age, and Ivy and I had a case to wrap up.

"Ready, partner?"

Ivy hesitated, fiddling with her lock. "Are you sure everything's in place?"

"Yes," I said. "What's up?"

She kept an eye on the sidewalk, watching for our target.

"What if Delia has a better plan?"

It was the same question I'd been asking myself all night. I kept coming up with the same answer. "I'm putting money on our plan over anything Delia can come up with."

"We're putting our trust in a lot of shady people," she pointed out.

"Yes," I said. "But we know they're shady, and they're giving us just the right amount of leverage. Did you check in with everyone this morning?"

She nodded. "They're still in."

"See?" I said to myself as much as Ivy. "Our plan is good. It follows the rules. We've got our people in place. All that's left is—"

"Actually pulling it off?"

"Exactly," I said.

"You're sure he'll show up?"

"Positive," I said. "Then we'll have her in the bag." I pulled a pack of Juicy out of my pocket and passed it to Ivy. She popped out a piece before gesturing across the yard with the pack.

"Incoming," she said.

I spotted Tim and Carl hovering by the walkway. "Right on time." Ivy stayed in position by the racks while I went over to speak with our hired muscle.

"Gentlemen."

"Howie," Tim said. "Fancy meeting you out here in the yard for no particular reason whatsoever."

Carl groaned softly.

You get what you pay for.

"Here they come." Carl managed the heads-up without moving his lips while Tim whipped around to look. Delia and Meredith were laboring up the sidewalk, carrying a large box.

"Should I bother reminding you that this is all fake?" I rolled my shoulders and secured my backpack.

"Sure," Tim said, cracking his knuckles. "But we'd hate for it to be unconvincing."

He put me in a headlock and lugged me over to the sidewalk. I was walking blind, but Carl was good enough to direct from a safe distance. "Look out for that rock. Now there's a dip. Tim, let him breathe."

Halfway down the sidewalk, I tapped Tim's arm. "Here's good." He released me, and I staggered as the blood flow returned to my brain.

"Can't stop now," Tim said. With an ease that could only be attributed to lifelong practice, he and Carl began shoving me around.

"Watch where you're going, Howie." Tim grabbed me by the collar and tossed me over to Carl. "What did we tell you about getting in our way?" I nearly face-planted before Carl caught me by the elbow and nudged me back toward Tim.

"Put some oomph into it, Carl," I whispered. He shrugged.

"Remember that you asked for it, Howard."

One big push sent me flailing into the box Delia and Meredith were holding. All three of us went down, and the box went flying.

"Howard!" Meredith yelled.

"How is this my fault?" I asked from my prone position on the ground.

"Are you guys okay?" Ivy came rushing over as Tim and Carl skulked back into the shadows. "What a couple of jerks."

I risked a peek at my partner. She was helping Delia up and winked at me while grabbing Delia's bag.

Pulling myself up, I spotted the most unexpected of treats on the sidewalk: a little white spaceman. Meredith and Delia were busy bemoaning the state of their space diorama, and Ivy was flitting about helping to pick up the rest of their stuff.

I whipped open my bag and stuffed Spaceman Joe inside. Dusting off my pants, I sidled up to the girls. "Everyone okay?" Meredith and Delia glowered at me while Ivy gave a thumbs-up.

"Whatever you're up to, it won't work." Delia was at my side, hissing in my ear.

"I guess we're going to have to find out," I whispered back before turning to Meredith and Ivy. "Meredith, you good?"

"No, I'm not *good*, Howard," she yelled. "Our project is—"

"Great, happy to hear it." We had to move this show along. "Sorry about that."

"We should go, bell's going to ring," Ivy said. "Can't be late."

I hustled inside without a backward glance. "All set?" If she hadn't managed to complete her part, our odds of success were sliding down to zero.

"Mission accomplished," Ivy said. "Glad that part's over."

"You and me both. Time for phase two."

... .− −− −..−. ... .−−. .− −.. .

Ivy and I sat waiting in our classroom, antsy with anticipation. Including so many people in the plan added an uncomfortable level of unpredictability. I was used to working with a party of one, and I always held up my end of the bargain. The emergency alliance we'd thrown together last night was shakier than Blue attempting a speed bump. I passed the time by imagining the thousands of ways this could go wrong.

There was a crackle over the loudspeaker as the morning

announcements began. Our illustrious president had been on board last night, but this was the moment of truth.

Mrs. Rodriguez opened with her list of announcements.

"And now here's Lisa Grantley with today's student news."

"Good morning, Grantleyville Middle School," Lisa said. "As your president, it is my duty to keep our school safe and free from corruption—to root out injustice and bring it to light."

I snuck a glance at Ivy. Her eyes were as big as saucers, and she smothered a laugh.

Lisa was on board all right.

"So, it is with a heavy heart that I tell you we have a traitor in our midst." Kids around us began shifting in their seats, murmuring to each other, and Ms. Kowalski sat up straight in her chair. "Delia Potts has stolen the council checks and is using them to blackmail our treasurer, Meredith Reddy, into leaving the council."

The noise level rose as Lisa's declaration began to sink in. I could hear Mrs. Rodriguez speaking up in the background.

Lisa was arguing with her. "The students need to know—"

Her voice cut off abruptly. High-pitched screeching erupted from the classroom next door. If I wasn't mistaken, someone was shouting my name.

Our own class had devolved into chaos. Kids were piled

together, sharing theories about what was really going on. Ms. Kowalski tried to settle everyone down, but it was useless. Nobody could remember the last time something this exciting had happened at G.M.S.

The speaker crackled back to life, and Mrs. Rodriguez's voice came through loud and clear. "I need to see the following students in my office immediately: Delia Potts, Meredith Reddy, Bradley Chen, Ivy Mason, and—" She paused for a weary sigh. "—Howard Wallace."

Chapter Twenty-Nine

The number of guilty parties involved meant we couldn't squeeze into Mrs. Rodriguez's office, so we were neatly packed into the teacher's lounge, a poorly lit room that smelled of burnt coffee. We sat on hard plastic chairs and waited for the parents to arrive. The teachers were playing things close to the vest, but the most telling bit of news was when we were told to bring our bags. Someone was getting suspended today.

I sat beside Ivy, trying to avoid the flaming daggers Delia's eyes were shooting at me from across the table. Meredith was next to her, furiously whispering in her ear while Bradley and Lisa made their case to Mrs. Rodriguez and Mr. Vannick.

"I still don't understand why I'm here," Lisa said. "I brought the problem to your attention."

"I'm not discussing this with you right now, Lisa," Mrs. Rodriguez said.

The door squeaked open, allowing a slender man with wire-rimmed glasses to slip into the room. He picked his way through the crowd and chose a seat beside my mother.

"Who's that?" I leaned over to whisper at Ivy.

"My dad."

I couldn't have stopped my double take if I had tried. "Didn't you say your dad was a cop? He looks like an accountant."

"That would be because he's an accountant," Ivy said. "I told you he was a cop so you'd let me be your partner."

I never knew you could be proud and annoyed in equal measure.

"How'd you do it, Howard?" Delia leaned across the table, hissing at me under the flood of conversation and ruining my moment. "How'd you get Lisa to turn?"

"Same way you got her involved in your little scheme," I said. "Appealing to her ego."

"We told her there was still a way to end up on top of this mess," Ivy said.

"If she was the one who discovered your crimes," I said. "And she was the one who exposed them . . ."

"Then she would be the hero who saved the school," Ivy finished.

"All future dances will be dedicated to Lisa." I swept a hand through the air, and Ivy checked off an imaginary box. "She'll have a drink named after her at the coffee bar."

"Probably a statue someday," Ivy said dreamily.

Delia looked over at Lisa in disgust. "What an idiot. She's been in this mess from the beginning. If I go down, she's coming with me."

"That's the plan," I said. On paper, anyway.

When everyone's parent representative was finally accounted for, Mrs. Rodriguez sat down at the head of the table. "This is a fine mess," she said. "Howard, why don't you start with all the information you neglected to share with us on Friday."

Delia was on her in an instant, holding up a hand. "Why does he get to go first?"

Mrs. Rodriguez paused long enough that even I felt uncomfortable. "Excuse me?"

"I'm the one being accused." Delia shifted in her seat. "Shouldn't I get to defend myself?"

This was an interesting change of pace. I hadn't expected Delia to be so bold. Her twelve hours of planning must have paid off as well. I eyed the clock. A Delia-sized roadblock would slow things down nicely, and I could use the extra time for phase three. There was also the added benefit that I would appear to be the kind and generous party.

"I don't mind if she goes first," I said, the very picture of selflessness.

Mrs. Rodriguez shot me a look. "I'm glad you approve."

"I can't believe I even have to say this, but I've done nothing wrong," Delia said. "I would never hurt my friend like that."

Meredith didn't look too confident about the truth of that statement.

"It's obviously a cry for attention from Howard," Delia continued. "He prides himself on knowing all this P.I. stuff, including breaking into lockers. He must have stolen the checks himself so he could have a big case."

"That'd be a shoddy way to run a business," I said.

"I bet you brought the checks with you as 'evidence.'"

Ah. That was her game. She must have realized we took the checks from her room and thought she could spin it to her advantage. Not today.

"Search his bag," Delia said. "That'll put an end to this right now."

Mrs. Rodriguez shook her head. "Delia, I—"

"It's okay," I said, holding out my bag. "You can look."

"Mine, too," Ivy said.

"It might move things along," Mrs. Rodriguez said. "Mr. Vannick, would you please?"

He didn't have to be asked twice. Mr. Vannick lifted our bags onto the table and dug in. He found fifteen packs of gum between the two of us, but no checks. The level of sheer disappointment radiating from him was heartbreaking. This was already turning out better than I'd hoped.

Delia had had her fair shake, and now it was time for the main event. I tucked my bag under my chair. "May I speak?"

"Go ahead," Mrs. Rodriguez said over Delia's protests.

"Last week Meredith hired me to find the missing student council checks and figure out who was blackmailing her," I said. Meredith nodded in agreement while the adults sat forward in their seats. They knew we were getting to the good stuff.

"I took Ivy on as a partner at the same time."

"Junior," Ivy said as she waved to the crowd.

"Bradley was our first suspect, but through our investigation, we realized he wasn't capable of acting alone."

Bradley stood up, mouth open to speak, but Lisa hauled him back down.

"Then," Ivy said. "We suspected Lisa, but she was way

too hot-headed to be the mastermind of such a cold-hearted scheme."

"Somebody else was pulling the strings," I said. "They were merely the lackeys."

Lisa pushed her chair back. "Why you dirty, double-crossing little—"

"Lisa," her mother said sharply. Our president turned red and ducked down in her chair with a frown.

"Yes," I said, grinning widely. "All of that and more."

"You said if I helped you, you'd keep me out of it," Lisa muttered.

I looked at Ivy. "Is that what I said?"

"No," Ivy said. "I don't think so."

"No, what I said was if you helped me, I'd make sure you got the recognition you deserve. Not my fault how you interpreted that."

"What have I told you about the fine print?" Mrs. Grantley snapped at her daughter.

"If you didn't write it, don't sign it," Lisa intoned.

"This was a rookie mistake," Mrs. Grantley said. "Your father's going to be very disappointed in you."

Lisa's face fell, and when she looked up at me, I knew she'd decided exactly where the blame belonged. I could only deal with one personal grudge at a time, so she'd have to get in line.

Mrs. Rodriguez attempted to redirect our focus. "Howard, back to the topic at hand, please?"

"Of course," I said. "In the case of Mr. Vannick, we had our reasons to suspect him, but we know how that turned out, so let's move on."

"Sorry, again," Ivy said, and Mr. Vannick grunted.

"They're stalling," Delia said, understanding sparking in her eyes. "Why are they stalling?"

With impeccable timing that I'd planned, but expected to fail miserably, a commotion started outside the door. Raised voices in the hallway wound their way through the lounge. I spotted Ms. Tomarelli's head through the window in the door as she attempted to block whoever was trying to get through. The office administrator was putting up a valiant fight.

"Sir, I told you," she said. "You cannot go in there."

"And I'm telling you I gotta see Mrs. Rodriguez." Marvin's foghorn voice squashed any further arguments. "This is important information she needs to know."

He burst through the door and strutted in like a proud rooster. "Which one of you is Mrs. Rodriguez?"

"I am." Mrs. Rodriguez stood, unsure of what to make of the wizened old man who stood before her. "Who are you?"

"Marvin Parsons of Marvin's on Main," Marv said, pumping her hand up and down. "Nice to meet you."

"Why—" Mrs. Rodriguez tried to get a word in, but Marvin was on a roll.

"I hate to tell you this, but you got a real problem with the kids at this school. One of them tried to make a purchase at my store with this." He handed her a check. "I highly doubt that was an authorized usage."

She examined the check. "Could you identify the student?"

Marvin scratched at his ear. "Yeah, probably." He glanced over at me, and I subtly pointed at Delia.

"Oh, hey," Marv said, examining the kids at our table. "It was that girl right there."

All eyes in the room turned to Delia.

"What?" she squawked. "I've never seen this man before in my life!"

"Are you calling me a liar?" Agitation had Marvin's voice shaking. "This is what I get for trying to do a good deed. Taking time away from my shop to come all the way over here."

"But it *is* a lie."

"I won't stand for this harassment. I'm telling it like it is. I saw you with my own two eyes in my shop with a fistful of checks."

Delia leapt up from the table. "That's impossible. They never left my room!"

The room went dead silent. Delia gasped and slapped a hand over her mouth.

Everything erupted at once.

Delia was yelling at me, Meredith was yelling at Delia, and Lisa was yelling at everyone. Mrs. Rodriguez was attempting to wrestle back control of the situation, but first she had to cut through the line of parents asking her how she let this happen and what she was going to do about it.

Marvin used the chaos to make his escape. He flashed two fingers at me before slipping out the door. Busting Delia so thoroughly was definitely worth owing Marvin a second favor.

Mrs. Rodriguez finally got the room settled down.

I cleared my throat. "I think it's only fair, given the evidence, that Delia's bag is searched as well."

The bag in question was set on the table while we all gathered round. Mr. Vannick did the honors again. He searched the bag inside out and found nothing until he came across a small side pocket. Mr. Vannick unzipped it to reveal the checks nestled inside.

"You put those in there," Delia said. "You stole them from my room on Sunday."

My mother turned to look at me. "I thought you were at Ivy's on Sunday."

I knew that story was going to come back to bite me eventually. "We may have taken a detour and done some investigating."

"Oh, Howard."

"It had to be done," I said. Of that, I had no doubt.

"More importantly," Ivy said as everyone returned to their seats, "have you guys been listening? I believe we have what's called a confession. Delia took the checks!"

Meredith shook her head. "But why?"

"I had no choice," Delia said, bitterness hanging on to every word. "You were leaving me behind. Everything was 'student council,' 'twenty-year plan,' 'eyes on the prize.'"

"But we're friends."

"Is that what you'd call us?" Delia scoffed. "Ever since you got elected, you've been ignoring me. When you did notice me, you were mean and bossy."

"So you decided to blackmail me." Meredith sat back in her chair, stunned.

"If you were off the council," Delia said. "We'd have a shot at being friends again. And if not friends, at least you'd be hurting too."

It sounded just as crazy the second time around. "I still think your logic is messed up," I said.

"Oh, be quiet, Howard," Delia snarled. "You ruined everything. I had the perfect plan. Lisa and Bradley were on board. Then you showed up and stuck your nose in it."

"I was hired to stick my nose in it."

"But nobody thought you'd be good at it." Lisa and Bradley nodded in vigorous agreement.

"I'm going to choose to take that as a compliment," I said.

"Taking the high road," my mother whispered behind me.

"We thought you'd fizzle out after a day," Delia said. "But you started closing in on us, and you had to be dealt with."

Another piece clicked into place. "That's why you went after Blue," I said.

"I had to do something to get you off my back."

"By slicing up a defenseless bike?"

My mother gasped, and the rest of the parents shifted uncomfortably. "You didn't tell us that," she said.

"I was handling it," I said. "There're always risks in my line of work. I just never thought anyone would be low enough to go after Blue."

"For the record," Delia said. "It might have been my idea, but Bradley and Lisa did the actual slicing and dicing."

Bradley sunk down in his chair, and Lisa leaned forward. "It's all going on the record, Delia," she said. "I'm not forgetting any of this."

"That makes two of us," Delia shot back.

"I still can't believe it was you," Meredith said.

"Why?" Delia stood up to pace beside her friend. "Because I should have rolled over like I always do? Let you get away with kicking me to the curb?"

"Here's a wild idea," Meredith sniped back. "You could have tried *talking* to me." She threw up her hands in exasperation when Delia snorted at that suggestion.

"In any case," Ivy said. "Turning to a life of crime should always be a last resort."

"Excellent point, partner." I nodded.

"Shut it, Howard Wallace." Delia and Meredith spoke as one poisonous unit.

"Well," I said to Ivy, "at least they agree on something."

"Warms the heart, doesn't it?" she said, patting a hand against her chest.

"Enough," Mrs. Rodriguez said. "Delia, sit down."

Lisa stood up. "I—"

"I'll deal with you in a minute, Lisa." Mrs. Rodriguez rubbed at her temples.

"Thank you, Howard and Ivy," she said eventually, "for bringing this to light."

Ivy and I nodded, proud of our accomplishment, yet humble.

"This does not change the fact that you weren't to be conducting your investigations on school property." I knew this was coming. No good deed goes unpunished, as they say. Especially when you break the rules to do the deed.

"Ivy, due to your involvement, you will join Howard for his detentions."

That was fair. Solidarity was good for a partnership.

"And Howard," she continued. "You can add an extra two weeks on to your detention thanks to your flagrant disregard for the rules."

"Only fitting for a senior partner," Ivy whispered, and I stifled a laugh. Our case had landed sunny-side up, and I still had my partner by my side. I could survive a little extra detention.

Ivy and I were excused, and Mrs. Rodriguez turned to Lisa, Bradley, Delia, and Meredith. "Now," she said. "What to do with you four?" My mother and Ivy's father prodded us out of the room.

I stuck my head back in before they closed the door.

"Before I forget, I'll be sending you the bill for Blue's new tires."

My mother dragged me down the hall and gave me a big hug. From the bowels of defeat, we had emerged victorious. I didn't bother to hide my smile.

Pulling back, she stared into my eyes. "I had no idea how much work you put into this job."

"Neither did I," Ivy's father said, shooting a wry look at his daughter. He stuck out a hand to my mother. "Hector Mason."

"Lois Wallace," my mother said, shaking his hand. She raised an eyebrow at me and Ivy. "Pity we couldn't have met under less detention-filled circumstances."

Mr. Mason laughed and nodded. "At least I finally got to meet the famous Howard Wallace."

"I don't know what he's talking about," Ivy said, grabbing her father's hand. "Come on, Dad, I'll walk you to your car."

"Good idea," he said. "You can fill me on all these interesting activities you've neglected to tell me about. Did Grandma know about this?"

Watching Ivy walk down the hall, trying to wriggle her way out of further punishment, I felt a pair of eyes on me. My mother was staring again.

"What?"

She smiled. "I like Ivy. She seems like a sweet girl."

"That's because you don't know her very well," I said.

Strolling down the hall, Ma laughed. "I guess we'll have to have her over for dinner, then."

The woman did not know what she was getting herself into. "We'll see," I said.

"I probably shouldn't say this," she said, putting an arm around my shoulder and drawing me in close. "But that was kind of fun."

"Getting hauled in front of the principal again?"

"No, that was bad. Don't repeat that," she said, frowning and then ruffling my hair. "But watching you in action? Pretty amazing."

Hope sprung up immediately. "Amazing enough that I'm unpunished?"

"Oh, no," she said. "You're still punished. And you've got a second grounding coming to you for violating the first."

"I'm sorry," I said. "Ivy and I had to finish it."

We walked along in silence, and I tried to figure out my next move. My mother seemed to be immersed in her own seriously deep thoughts.

She cleared her throat before I could speak. "You made some mistakes this week, Howard, and broke many, many rules."

That was undeniable.

"But," she continued, "I think your father and I may have made a mistake, too."

I stopped breathing. All my energy was being put into listening to my mother's next words.

"You and Ivy risked a lot to solve this case and make things right. The two of you are quite the team," she said. "I think banning something you're so passionate about was not the best solution."

The sweet air of victory began to fill my lungs. Fingers crossed that Pete had managed to keep my pickle buckets.

"Don't jump to any conclusions about getting off easy, but I'll speak to your father when he gets home," Ma said as she laced her fingers through mine. "Perhaps we need to reevaluate the terms of your sentence."

Chapter Thirty

Sometimes, enthusiasm and perseverance can outweigh a bad decision. At least, it did for my folks. Pops was as impressed as my mother was with how doggedly I went after Meredith's case, even after I'd been expressly forbidden. They didn't want to stifle my investigative instincts, but there were strict conditions to operate under. I had to promise to check in with them and conduct my business responsibly. And I had to reduce my hours. I'd need a sign that read:

Wallace Investigations (Saturday, Sunday, and every other Friday).

That night, Pops visited the back office while I filed Medith's paperwork. "Your mom and I tried to get rid of this, but we couldn't bring ourselves to do it." He passed me a brown lump. "You can't be out investigating without it."

My coat, better and browner than ever.

"Thanks, Pops." Now I was officially back in business.

"Also, we got you something." He brought his arm out from behind his back and handed me a dusty, black oval box. "Open it." I pulled off the lid and dug through the tissue paper.

"It's for Christmas, but we decided to give it to you now since it seemed appropriate."

Inside the box was a worn, brown fedora. Lovingly worn, not shabbily. And it fit perfectly. My old man nodded in satisfaction. "Marvin said that one would do." Good old Marvin. Pops snapped his fingers and reached into his pocket. "Almost forgot. He also asked me to give you this." He passed me an envelope with my name written in spidery scrawl across it.

I opened it up to find a Marvin's on Main Street receipt inside.

Howard, come and see me this week. We got to talk about that first favor you owe me.

Marvin

P.S. Wear the hat.

Yup. Good old Marvin.

"Knock, knock." Ivy poked her head in through the doorway.

"Hey, Ivy," my old man said. He moved toward the door to leave.

"Thanks, Pops," I said. "This is perfect." He smiled at me and headed back into the house.

"Back in the office," Ivy said. "How's it feel?"

I leaned back in my chair. "Feels good."

Ivy plopped down in the cozy chair, remembered the stink, and got back up. "Did you get Spaceman Joe back to Kevin? Is he surviving the wrath of Delia after helping us?"

"Kevin was very pleased," I said. "He appeared to still be in one piece, but the fact that Delia's not allowed out of her room—"

"And he's not allowed in it—" Ivy smiled as she leaned against my desk.

"—definitely helped with that." I grabbed the last of Meredith's paperwork and stuffed it into her file. Ivy took the file and shoved it into the cabinet. I made a mental note to search for it later since I was 98 percent sure she put it in a random spot.

"I'm still peeved that Bradley and Lisa got off so lightly," Ivy said.

I shrugged. "Deep pockets have a way of filling any holes you've gotten yourself into." Lisa's parents' pockets went on for miles. They'd sent me money for Blue's repairs, but I felt skeezy using it. Grantley money had to be ill-gotten gains. I decided to keep it aside for an emergency bribes fund.

"At least that's one campaign promise fulfilled," Ivy said. "The coffee bar will make a lovely addition to the teacher's lounge."

"Once again, everything comes up Grantley."

"So, things are back to normal," Ivy said. "What's our new case? What're we working on?"

"Leaves," I said. I walked out into the yard and Ivy followed.

"Huh?"

"We're allowed to keep the business going, but my folks aren't going to let my punishment slide. They've assigned me chores. Lots of chores," I said. "Starting with leaves."

Ivy picked up a rake that had been propped against the office wall. "And I take it you'd like my help?"

I grinned and grabbed the second rake. She sighed and started raking. There was something to be said for having a partner again. I clapped a hand on her shoulder. "You're a good man, sister."

Ivy looked up and smiled. "*Maltese Falcon*, right?"

"You watched the movies!"

She shook a finger at me and looked stern. "I completed my

training regimen," she said. I laughed and went back to work. Leaning against her rake handle, Ivy eyed me contemplatively.

"When did you get a hat?" she asked. "I should get a hat."

I tipped the hat off my head and eyed it, considering, before plopping it back into place.

"Hats are for senior partners only."

"Okay, seriously?" Ivy managed to glare and roll her eyes at me in one go.

"Dead serious," I said. "We'll go see Marvin tomorrow and check out his stock."

A huge grin swept across her face, and she did a little dance with the rake. "Now you're talking. Mason and Wallace—"

"Wallace and Mason," I said. "Let's not get crazy."

"Whatever," Ivy said. "Wallace and Mason Investigations— '*we keep a file, so you don't have to.*'"

"That our new slogan?"

"Would you prefer 'we hide in closets, so you don't have to'?" Ivy tapped her chin. "Or 'Stealth, surveillance, and secrecy are our guarantee'? I actually like that one. That's a serious suggestion."

We'd work on it. But a new slogan for a new team sounded good.

Even if it meant new sticky notes.

Wallace and Mason Investigations

Mason and Wallace Investigations

Rules of Private Investigation

1. Work with what you've got. Especially when it's a fabulous shade of green.
2. Ask the right questions.
3. Know your surroundings.
4. Always have a cover story ready.
5. Blend in.
6. A bad plan is better than no plan. I think we need to revisit this rule. —No.
7. Never underestimate your opponent.
8. Never tip your hand.
9. Don't get caught. You should try following this rule, Howard.
10. Pick your battles. Stop it.
11. Don't leave a trail.
12. Everyone has a hook.
13. Always listen to your partner. She's a genius.

Speaking of rules we need to revisit.
Very funny.

Acknowledgments

A huge amount of people had a hand in *Howard Wallace, P.I.* becoming a real, live book. I've been lucky to work with some of the kindest, most supportive, and talented folks. Howard and I wouldn't be here without them. Get your cheers ready!

To my phenomenal agent, Molly Ker Hawn: Thank you for choosing to work your special brand of smart, fierce, and funny magic with me. You're amazing, and I'm forever grateful to have you in my corner.

To my delightful editor, Christina Pulles: Working with you has been everything I hoped for and more. It's been a pleasure to be partnered up with such a fun, smart, and kind individual. Thank you for picking me and Howard!

To the incredible people at Sterling: I've been in the best hands throughout this entire, amazing experience. Your enthusiasm and support at every turn has been a beautiful gift. Many heartfelt thanks to Hanna Otero, Theresa Thompson, Kim Broderick, Brian Phair, Fred Pagan, Scott Amerman, Merideth Harte, Sari Lampert, Lauren Tambini, Josh Redlich, Ardi Alspach, Chris Vaccari, Trudi Bartow, and the fantastic sales team.

A special shout-out to designer Andrea Miller for the best page breaks in any book ever.

Thank you to all my friends who've read various versions of *Howard* along the way: Steph L., Stephanie B. and Gabe, Leanne S., Jody D., Jane G., as well as my teen readers Victoria G., Alana H., and Shey-Lyn R. Many thanks to Wade Albert White, Joy McCullough, and K. Kazul Wolf as well.

Thank you to everyone at Kick-Butt Kidlit, the Sweet Sixteens, and Pitch Wars for widening my circle with your friendship and camaraderie.

To the marvelous Sarah LaPolla: Thank you for being so kind to a petrified newbie author at her first conference. Your feedback and encouragement was appreciated beyond measure.

To my incredible critique partners: Naomi Hughes (my

Pitch Wars Obi-Wan), Kendra Young, Wendy Parris, and Laura Shovan: Thank you for being there through the wails and cheers. You are extraordinary women whom I'm fortunate to know and beyond lucky to call my friends.

To my amazing boss, Jean Moir: Your support and enthusiasm have allowed me to work both of my dream jobs, and I'm forever grateful for that. Thank you to everyone at the Middlesex County Library for cheering me on and being the most excellent friends and coworkers.

To my fantastic family and friends: I consider it the best kind of problem that there are far too many of you to name here. Thank you for always being excited to hear what's new and for your endless enthusiasm and encouragement.

To my grandmas, Patt and Elaine: Thank you for being the kind of grandmothers who always encouraged their grandkids to go after their dreams.

To my outstanding sisters, Jordan and Aidan: You are two of my biggest cheerleaders, and I've loved sharing this adventure with you. Thank you for your love, support, and endless happy dances.

To my truly wonderful parents: My heart is overflowing with love and gratitude. I wish I could list everything you've done for me so everyone would know exactly how amazing you are. None of this would be happening without your support and encouragement. Thank you for teaching our family to cherish and embrace our creativity. Thank you for providing me with the space not only to grow but also to flourish. And thank you for always thinking I could do this.

And finally to Past!Casey: Thanks for deciding to go for it. High fives.